J. M. Jephson, Ernest Edwards

Shakespere

his birthplace, home, and grave - a pilgrimage to Stratford-on-Avon in the autumn

of 1863

J. M. Jephson, Ernest Edwards

Shakespere

his birthplace, home, and grave - a pilgrimage to Stratford-on-Avon in the autumn of 1863

ISBN/EAN: 9783337287047

Printed in Europe, USA, Canada, Australia, Japan

Cover: Foto ©Andreas Hilbeck / pixelio.de

More available books at **www.hansebooks.com**

SHAKESPERE:

HIS BIRTHPLACE, HOME, AND GRAVE.

SHAKESPERE:

HIS BIRTHPLACE, HOME, AND GRAVE.

A Pilgrimage to Stratford-on-Avon

IN THE AUTUMN OF 1863.

BY THE

REV. J. M. JEPHSON, B.A., F.S.A.

WITH

PHOTOGRAPHIC ILLUSTRATIONS BY ERNEST EDWARDS, B.A.

A Contribution to the Tercentenary Commemoration of the Poet's Birth.

LONDON:

LOVELL REEVE & CO., 5, HENRIETTA STREET,

COVENT GARDEN.

1864.

PRINTED BY
JOHN EDWARD TAYLOR, LITTLE QUEEN STREET,
LINCOLN'S INN FIELDS.

PREFACE.

—0—

FOUR years ago I was induced to give a very plain, matter-of-fact account of a tour which I took in Brittany. To my great furprife and pleafure it was moft indulgently received by my literary friends, the critics. I accomplifhed, not only my primary object of paffing my fummer holiday with pleafure and profit, but alfo the fecondary one of obtaining much unexpected praife. I have been ever fince projecting another expedition, but fomething always prevented me, till laft autumn, when my friend, Mr. Lovell Reeve, fuggefted a vifit to Stratford-upon-Avon, and a little book à propos of the Tercentenary Feftival in honour of Shakefpere's birth. A love for the drama, and an efpecial veneration for the Father of it in England, are, I may fay, hereditary in my family. In the laft century my grand-uncle, Robert Jephfon, was one of thofe who endeavoured to revive the romantic drama of the Elizabethan era, and wrote feveral tragedies, amongft which was "The Count of Narbonne," founded on Walpole's " Caſtle of Otranto," and " Julia, or the Italian Lovers," which long held poſſeſſion of the ſtage. From my childhood, then, I have heard Shakeſpere diſcuſſed, extolled, acted, and quoted; and I was glad of an opportunity of viſiting the place which is eſpecially conſecrated to his memory, and of adding my tiny grain to the volume of incenſe which will riſe in his honour on his three hundredth birthday. The few facts of his life already known have been publiſhed over and over again ; but I thought that they might be ſo connected with the ſcene of his youth and the choſen retreat of his mature age, as to make a whole which might be ſuggeſtive of thought to thoſe who ſhall viſit Stratford next ſpring. I am the more bold to offer this little ſketch to lovers of England's greateſt poet, becauſe, if, like Moſes, my ſpeech be weak and ſtammering, I am aſſiſted by a coadjutor whoſe camera is almoſt as great a worker of wonders as was Aaron's rod.

CONTENTS.

—o—

CHAPTER I.

CHAPTER II.

CHAPTER III.

CHAPTER X.

CHAPTER XI.

CHAPTER XII.

LIST OF PHOTOGRAPHIC ILLUSTRATIONS.

—o—

SHAKESPERE.

****

CHAPTER I.

MANY are the changes which have paſſed over England ſince Edward the Third was king; and amongſt
them not the leaſt characteriſtic is that which may be
obſerved in the objects, the manner, and the ſeaſons of
our pilgrimages. The men of the fourteenth century
ſought forgetfulneſs of the evils under which they
groaned by adoring at the ſhrine of the bold prieſt
who, by paſſive reſiſtance, withſtood the will of the
fierce Norman Conqueror; we try to elevate our minds
above the common drudgery of life by ſeeking Nature
where ſhe may be worſhipped in her grandeſt forms,
or by treading the ground which has been conſecrated
by Genius. They rode from every ſhire's end of
England to kneel at the ſhrine of Beckett, "the holy,
bliſsful martyr," and to kiſs his blood-ſtained veſtments;
we take the expreſs train to Warwick, and thence

proceed by omnibus to Stratford-upon-Avon, that we may gaze on the cottage where Shakefpere was born and the grave where his bones moulder in peace. Their minds were prepared to adore in the gorgeous temple where the relics of the faint were enfhrined in gold and precious ftones, by the perufal of legends written in defiance of Nature and Tafte ; our intereft in the homely fcenes we vifit is infpired by poems in which Nature is prefented to our minds with the fidelity of the moft confummate art, and every fenti-ment and word dictated by the moft exquifite tafte. Not lefs fignificant is the change in the feafon at which we feek our annual recreation. In days when men were content with few luxuries and had leifure to choofe their time for work and play, the verdure, the flowers, the finging of the birds, and the genial breezes of April, reminded them that a ride in pleafant com-pany through the pretty fields and woods of Kent would be beneficial to their fouls ; then " longen folk to gon on pilgrimages ;" now we can only fave from labour and corroding cares a few weeks at the fag end of fummer, when we are releafed for a feafon from the confuming toils of our bufy life.

On the whole, I think our nineteenth-century pil-grimages, whether their objects be the Matterhorn or the little town of Stratford-upon-Avon, have the

advantage of their predeceffors in the fourteenth century. But in one refpect mine was fadly inferior to that
which ftarted from the *Tabard* in the Borough fomewhere about the year 1383. I had no " perfight gentil
knight," no clerk of Oxenford, no jolly friar, no gentle
manciple, no gallant fquire, no precife priorefs, no boifterous hoft, to bear me company; nor, I fear, if I had,
fhould I have anfwered to the defcription of the " pore
perfoun of a toun" in any quality except that implied
in the firft epithet. " I rode all unarmed and I rode all
alone." I rode becaufe I preferred fpending my " parfon's week" loitering among the green lanes, taking
the rough and fmooth, the funfhine and fhower, the
bitter and fweet, as it pleafed God to fend them, to being
whifked from one point of my journey to the other
in a railway carriage. In the latter plan the journey
itfelf is quite uninterefting, and is, therefore, hurried
over as quickly as poffible; in the former it forms part
of the pleafure of the trip. " The prize is in the purfuit." Some of my neighbours, indeed, to whom I imparted my defign, faid very plainly, by their looks at leaft,
that they thought me a trifle infane for fpending three
days in travelling a diftance which might be accomplifhed by train in as many hours; but the imputation
of infanity is one which muft be fubmitted to by any
one who refolves to follow his own inclinations in thefe

days when all thought and action are civilifed down
to a dead level of infipid conventionalifm.

A friend kindly lent me a Norwegian pony of fmall
fize but immenfe power, for the journey. Thefe ftrong,
compact little animals get through far more work than
a large horfe. I chriftened my temporary fervant
" Stornoway," for I thought that had a fine Scandinavian found. And fo, having packed the feweft poffible
number of neceffaries in the old knapfack which had
accompanied me round Brittany fome fix years ago, and
ftrapped it on little Stornoway's crupper, I mounted for
my journey.

At that moment, my black retriever, whom his
former mafter had called "Smoker," came bounding
up, wriggling from fide to fide, holding up " his honeft
bawfoned fonfie face," laying back his ears, and wag-
ging his tail, as much as to fay, " What a pleafant ride
we are going to have together." I did not like to
difappoint him, and it ftruck me that he might make
an agreeable addition to the *tête-à-tête* between me and
Stornoway. So Smoker was permitted to join the
expedition.

By the way, I never could make out the propriety
of calling a dog " Smoker." Johnfon explains the
word, " One who dries or perfumes by fmoke." And
with all his good qualities, Smoker is as guiltlefs as

Crab was of having anything in common with per-
fume. Smoker is not a romantic or an elegant name;
but my Smoker is as good-natured, fagacious, faithful,
engaging, and, I may fay, with *Launce*, "gentleman-
like" a dog, as if he had taken his name from gods
or heroes. Still, I muft fay, he had fome of Crab's
qualities, for he never fhed a tear at leaving his friends,
the beagle puppies.

The evening was delightful. It was the 31ft of
Auguft: every field was filled with labourers gathering
in the heavy fheaves, and at every turn I met the laden
waggons, drawn by their fturdy teams, and entering
the homefteads.

But, at the very outfet, I met with fome troubles
for which I had not bargained. Stornoway was a very
wife little fellow, and evidently thought that though
it might be very good fun for me to ride along the
pleafant lanes of England on a harveft evening on his
legs, he had much rather be in his comfortable ftable,
and that poffibly a little well-timed firmnefs on his part
might intimidate the new rider whom he found upon
his back. Accordingly, as foon as he came to the
well-known gate of his home he objected ftrongly to
go any farther. The fmalleft intimation of mine with
hand or knee that I wifhed him to go on, was met
with a defiant tofs of the head. When I became im-

portunate he fidled towards the gate. But he immediately refented an application of the whip or fpur by
ftanding up ftraight on his hind-legs. If I had not
been very quick in leaning well forward and loofening
the reins, he muft have tumbled back on the hard road.
The next time he tried it, however, I was prepared, and
leaning over his fhoulder with a rein in each hand, I
pulled him down, and then applied the fpurs vigoroufly.
After fome fighting and lofs of time and temper on both
fides, we agreed upon a truce. The fame fcene was
repeated, however, with gradually diminifhed intenfity
at every farm-yard we came to, and I thought to myfelf, " Mafter Stornoway, either you muft give in, or we
fhall not reach Stratford this month." Stornoway *did*
give in, for this was the laft time he fhowed any ferious
difpofition to difpute my wifhes.

Hertford was my deftination on the firft night of
my pilgrimage, and my road lay through the pretty
village of Blackmore, and to the left of Foreft Hall,
whence many a gallant fox has broken covert, and
led the Effex hounds for miles acrofs the celebrated
Roding, or Roden, country, on the outfkirts of which
it is fituated. Both the country and the peer take
their titles from the little ftream called the Roden
which runs through it. About four miles on this fide
of Epping I turned to the right for Harlow Bufh, and

as the fhades of evening were defcending, paffed the
fine park of the Rev. Jofeph Arkwright, a brother-in-
law of the Bifhop of Rochefter, and Mafter of the Effex
Fox-hounds; and what is more, though now over
fixty, one of the fineft riders in England. From Harlow Bufh my way lay through Natfhall Crofs, Burnt
Mills, Eaftwich, and Stanftead—all charming, picturefque villages of thatched and tiled cottages, furrounded by trees. The moon had rifen, the ftars were
fhining, and the clocks were going nine as I faw the
lights of Hertford below me in the valley. I put up
at the *Dimfdale Arms*, and having feen Stornoway fed,
retired to what is called the coffee-room, having accomplifhed twenty-fix miles on this the firft day of
my pilgrimage.

Perhaps it may be ufeful to obferve that horfes on a
journey derive wonderful benefit from being fed in the
prefence of their mafters. Why it is I never could
make out; it may be that they enjoy their corn the
more for company. The coachman of a friend of
mine always makes it a point to comb his horfes' tails
while they are eating their oats at an inn, and he fays
that they do their work as well again in confequence
of this practice. The oftlers do not like it.

Having feen my pony fed, the next thing was to
look after my own creature comforts. And here I was

ſoon made unpleaſantly aware that I was travelling in a country where people live *at home.* I might have ſaid, it is true,

> "The chambres and the ſtables were wyde,
> And wel we weren eſud atte beſte,"

as far as houſe-room went ; but in reſpect of all that miniſters to real material comfort and cheerfulneſs, an Engliſh inn is far behind a Continental one. In a French town ſuch as Hertford, there would have been a *ſalle-à-manger* filled with gueſts, and the *chef* would have ſent in a refreſhing *potage,* with ſome delicate cutlets, or other *appétiſſant* diſh, followed by a *poire cuite,* and waſhed down with a bottle of Bordeaux. Here I was ſhown into a room, carpeted and curtained it is true, with well-ſtuffed chairs to ſit on or to go to ſleep in, but with an air as if it was never occupied. And then when I aſked for ſupper I was told I might have cold beef, or they would ſend out for a chop—a thing with a quantity of fat and griſtle on it, from which one has to pare the eatable part with the greateſt care, and even that is imbued with the flavour of the tallow which one has to baniſh to the farther corner of one's plate. And this is to be waſhed down with heavy brewer's ale or brandied ſherry. We Engliſh are indeed highly favoured in our meat, but who ſent us our cooks ?

While waiting for my animals to be fed next morning, I ſtrolled about the town. The ſtaple manufacture here is ſchoolboys. There are the Blue Coat School, the Green Coat School, and ever ſo many other ſchools, public and private, and upon theſe the tradespeople live. The town is ſurrounded by fine woods, and prettily ſituated on the river Lea, where the quaint old haberdaſher, Izaak Walton, uſed to catch chubs with toaſted cheeſe, and liſten to the milk-maids ſinging " Come live with me and be my love."

At about nine I ſtarted, intending to paſs through Welwyn, ſeven miles diſtant; Wheathampſtead, five miles from Welwyn, both in Hertfordſhire; Luton, eight miles from Wheathampſtead, in Bedfordſhire; Dunſtable, five miles from Luton; Leighton Buzzard, nine miles from Dunſtable; and perhaps Winſlow in Bucks, twelve miles from Leighton : thus making forty-ſix miles in the day. This would have been too long a journey for a continuance; but I thought that it would be beſt to get well forward towards my deſtination at firſt, and then to take my time afterwards; and little Stornoway did not ſeem to mind my weight in the leaſt.

On leaving Hertford, I took the wrong turning for Welwyn, but it proved a fortunate miſtake; for the road led me round Panſhanger, the beautiful demeſne of Lord Cowper. Happily it is furrounded by park-palings, not a wall, and I had an advantageous view of the green glades, dotted here and there with noble oaks and elms, and lofing themfelves in coppices of beech. Smoker put up feveral coveys of birds which lay funning themfelves and bathing in the duft by the road-fide; and by eleven o'clock I heard the guns going in all directions, and faw the fhooting parties " going a-birding," and tramping through the Swedes. It was a fplendid firft of September, if not for the par-tridges, at leaft for the fportfmen.

After paffing Panfhanger, I defcended into the valley of the Lea, along which the road runs for feveral miles. It is a fluggifh river, and is laid out at this part of its courfe in extenfive beds of water-creffes, which men were employed in gathering. Unfortunately it had no " fhingly bars," nor did it "chatter" as it went, but only " loitered " continually " round its creffes." To do it juftice, however, it did " ftir its fweet Forget-me-nots that grow for happy lovers," and indeed abounded with the richeft vegetation.

At Welwyn, a fplendid viaduct, of nearly a quarter of a mile long, fpans this valley, and carries the Great Northern Railway acrofs it. From this to Luton, which is fituated on the boundary between Herts and Beds, the road lies along the fluggifh ftream, and paffes to Luton Hoo, formerly belonging to the Marquis of Bute. A few years ago it was burnt down, and the ruins and eftate were purchaſed by a Liverpool attorney, who had made a fortune by the ſale of land at Birkenhead. Luton Hoo is ſurrounded by a great, high, ugly, brick wall, and threatening placards denounce the ſevereſt penalties of the law againſt thoſe who dare to tread its hallowed precinɑts ; ſo the attorney has his fine place all to himſelf. How different from the ſtately Panſhanger, with its picturefque park-pales, the fence of Engliſh demeſnes and warrens from time immemorial.

Luton is the head-quarters of the ſtraw bonnet manufaɑture, and has all the unpleaſing look of a manufaɑturing town.

After leaving Luton, I found that the country loſt its rich park-like charaɑter. The ſoil appears to be chalk, and the landſcape ſtretches away in fine breezy downs and rolling hills, and corn-fields of fifty acres in extent.

The entrance to Dunſtable—the place where the ſtraw bonnets were firſt manufaɑtured, and from whence they take their name, and where you now ſee women walking about platting, as they knit on the Continent—is very ſtriking. The church, an exquiſite example of Early Engliſh architeɑture, appear-

ing all the more beautiful from the uglinefs of the
furrounding buildings, ftands to the left. The deep
arcading and bold mouldings of the weft end are perfectly charming.

It is the fafhion, I believe, to fay that Gothic archi-
tecture culminated in the Decorated period, but to
me, judging merely by the light of nature without
any pretenfion to deep learning on the fubject, there
feems a poetry, a feeling in the Early Englifh which
the ftyle of no other period approaches.

Here I was ftruck by a name which appeared over
the door of a wretched public-houfe. It was Norman
Snoxell. What on earth could have brought Norman
Snoxell to Dunftable to retail beer and tobacco? Bal-
zac ufed to perambulate the ftreets of Paris for days
looking over the doors of the fhops for appropriate
names for his characters. Here would have been
quite a godfend for any novelift who wanted to name
his Norfe fmuggler or pirate. But, indeed, the names
of the Englifh peafantry are fometimes very curious.
I remember, in Norfolk, a fervant-maid named Phebe
Blanchflower. You would never expect fuch a name
out of a novel; but it was a real name neverthelefs;
for her father, old Blanchflower, drove the Ipfwich
mail for many years.

I reached Leighton Buzzard, on the borders of

Bucks, at about fix; but I was determined, if poffible, to fleep at Winflow where I heard there was a very comfortable country inn, and fo pufhed on; but both Stornoway and I were tired, and the laft five miles feemed interminable. However, at Winflow we arrived at about ten o'clock, and put up at the " Bell," having accomplifhed a journey of forty-fix miles fince breakfaft.

Next morning, being the 2nd of September, I ftarted from Winflow at a little after nine, purpofing, if poffible, to reach Edgehill the fame night. Edgehill is within twelve miles of Stratford, and I thought that by fleeping there, I might ride into Stratford next morning at my leifure, and thus have the advantage of feeing the end and object of my pilgrimage by daylight.

The firft town I reached was Buckingham, feven miles from Winflow. It is a nice, pretty country town, in the valley of the Stour. Between this and Brackley I paffed one of the lodges of Stowe, and then the fcenery changed. I am no great geologift, but the ftone appeared to me to be a reddifh green limeftone. It lies in regular ftrata, and comes out of the earth in nice rectangular pieces, well adapted for building. Accordingly the houfes and fences are all built of ftone, the latter having no mortar; but

great art is apparently employed in making the ftones
fit nicely into each other, and fome of the walls have
quite a Cyclopean or Etrufcan character. I was particularly ftruck with the village of Middleton-Cheney.
Here the houfes feem very old, and the brown and
greenifh ftone of which they are built has become
covered with lichens, which add much to the beauty
of the colouring. Their fhingled roofs, of high pitch,
are very picturefque. Yet here, where Nature and the
practice of former generations would feem to have
plainly indicated the right forms and materials, the
people are actually building fome new almfhoufes of
flaming red brick and blue flate. Red brick may be
made a very beautiful material, and is proper for London or Effex, where there is no ftone; but to import
it into a place where there is already a beautiful material provided by Nature, fhows a wonderful amount
of bad tafte in the builders.

Banbury is a handfome town, and the principal inn
extremely comfortable. I could not defcry the Crofs,
to which, when I was a baby, I was invited to " ride
a cock-horfe;" but I ate a Banbury cake out of curi-
ofity. It is a villainous invention, being a "roll-up,"
to ufe Mifs Evans' expreffion, of rich paftry, envelop-
ing currants.

From Banbury I ftarted at a little after fix, and,

after paffing fome gentlemen's places—Colonel North's amongft the reft—got upon fome high table-land, with wild country, as far as I could fee in the rapidly clof-ing-in evening, on either fide. Smoker as well as I feemed to feel the lonelinefs of the road, for inftead of foraging about as ufual, and enjoying the pleafure of finding out what everything he paffed fmelt of, he kept clofe to Stornoway's heels. At laft I faw a twinkling light, which I afterwards found proceeded from the houfe of a Mr. Fitzgerald, and defcried two keepers under the trees. This was quite a relief. Prefently I came to an almoft ruinous toll-bar, and in a few mi-nutes more reached the lonely road-fide inn. This was Edgehill, where the firft blood was drawn in the Civil War. I knocked at the door with my whip, and was anfwered by a fcared maid, who, however, foon made me comfortable; and I went to bed in a great, wild chamber, and dreamt of battles between Cavaliers and Roundheads, the latter being worfted by a well-directed fire of Enfield rifles, in which I took part.

CHAPTER II.

Next morning I found that the inn at which I had flept was called the " Sun Rifing." It bears on its walls the old proverb, " Good wine needs no bufh," yet betrays its unbelief in the adage by difplaying over the door a huge bunch of grapes.

It is built on the very edge of a fteep hill, hence probably called Edgehill, and commands a fine view of at leaft thirty miles in extent, bounded by the Malvern Hills. To the right is the village of Kyneton, or Kington, where the Parliamentary army was pofted on the eve of the battle of Edgehill; and clofe under the hill is Battle Farm, where the firft battle was fought in the quarrel between the Sovereign and the Parliament,

> " When hard words, jealoufies, and fears
> Set folks together by the ears."

But what was more to my prefent purpofe, mine hoft pointed out to me a little rifing ground in the middle of the vaft plain which was fpread out before me, behind which, he faid, lay Stratford-upon-Avon. Here, then, I was beginning to tread the ground which was familiar to him whofe words are houfehold words to all Englifh-fpeaking people, and which fuggefted to him thofe fweet, and withal accurate and life-like pictures of country manners with which his great poems abound.

At about ten o'clock I ftarted on my final ride to Stratford, and after defcending the almoft precipitous hill upon which the inn is perched, I found myfelf on a level road, bounded on either fide by cornfields, from which the harveft was, in many cafes, not yet gathered in. The only villages of note I paffed were Pillerton Priors and Eatington, the feat, ever fince the Conqueft, of the ancient family of Shirley.

At a little after twelve I came in fight of the beautiful old bridge built over the Avon at the entrance to Stratford, by Sir Hugh Clopton, in the reign of Henry VII. It confifts of fourteen flightly-pointed arches, and is nearly, if not quite, level. In fact, one does not fee how modern architects excel the older ones, even in this thoroughly utilitarian branch of the art—at leaft fo far as the old materials of lime and ftone are employed. The feudal *trinoda neceffitas* laid upon the vaffal the obligation of defending the country, building bridges, and keeping the highways in order, and the vaſſal appears to have performed the obligation tolerably well in mediæval England.

And now I was all expe𝜀tation. I had at laſt reached the ſpot where Shakeſpere was born, where he imbibed his earlieſt impreſſions from outward things, and where he choſe to ſpend his life, in preference to many other places which would ſeem to have had greater claims upon his regard. The queſtion I aſked myſelf was, Is it poſſible, by fixing my mind upon the ſcene which inſcribed its impreſſions upon the white paper of the poet's mind, and comparing it with his writings and with the few faɔts known of his life, to arrive at any-thing like a juſt conception of the man himſelf? I have often obſerved that by perſeveringly fixing the attention upon a difficult paſſage in a foreign language, the meaning after a time ſeems to flaſh like lightning upon the mind. Can I, by any proceſs like this, read the myſterious book of Shakeſpere's nature?

My firſt impreſſions were certainly not encouraging. The bridge was fine, and to the right was a pretty old houſe, approached by an avenue of trees, and kept with that beautiful neatneſs and elegance of greenſward and flower-beds which is ſeen nowhere but in England. The Avon, too, was flowing majeſtically on, as it did when Shakeſpere played upon its banks, or flew his hawk at the wild-fowl which harboured in its ſedges;

and a pair of ſwans, accompanied by their cygnets, were thruſting their long necks to the bottom, where they probably found an abundant repaſt of worms and grubs, waſhed down from ſome new cuts and embankments a little higher up the ſtream. Theſe were all pleaſing objects, upon which the fancy of a poet might delight to dwell; but as I rode up the High Street, I was obliged to acknowledge that Stratford is about as uninteresting to the outward ſenſes as any country town I had ever ſeen in England. There is no appearance of anything like antiquity, except perhaps a couple of carriers' inns, and they are moderniſed. There is no appearance even of wealth, nor any of that neatneſs and elegance which are its fruits. Stratford is a collection, generally ſpeaking, of mean houſes, and the High Street is not its beſt feature. At the upper extremity is the ugly market-houſe, where the old market-croſs uſed to ſtand, but this diſappeared in the laſt or the beginning of this century.

Having called at the " Red Horſe," a good inn on the right of the High Street, in hopes of finding that Mr. Edwards, the photographer, had arrived—a hope in which I was diſappointed—I turned to the left, down Chapel Street, to the " Shakeſpere," where I took up my quarters.

The " Shakeſpere " is an old-faſhioned, comfortable

inn, and the hoft fhows a laudable intereft in the Poet
who gives a name to his hoftelry and brings him moft
of his cuftomers. Each room is called after one of
the plays, the title of which is placed over the door.
Thus the commercial room is fuperfcribed "The
Tempeft"—not very appropriately, however, at leaft
during my ftay, for the houfe was remarkably quiet.
The coffee-room was "As You Like It"—I confefs I
did not much like it, for it was as lonely as the Foreft
of Arden itfelf. My bed-chamber was named "A
Midfummer Night's Dream;" another on the fame
landing, "Much Ado about Nothing;" another,
"Love's Labour Loft," and fo on. Bufts of the Poet
are placed on every lobby, and the walls are hung
with portraits of himfelf and illuftrations of his works.
A curious old clock, faid to have been taken from
New Place, and various articles of ancient furniture
with which his name is connected, are to be feen in
different parts of the houfe. Indeed, as a general rule,
I believe Stratford-upon-Avon may be faid to live
upon the memory of its great Poet, as Rome does
upon the relics of the Apoftles.

What a capital plan it would be, by the way, to fet
up a Shakefperian high-prieft at Stratford, whofe func-
tion it fhould be to regulate the devotions of the pilgrims and employ himfelf in the *culte des ruines*, and

who ſhould be inſpired to pronounce an infallible judgment upon Shakeſperian criticiſm. He ſhould decide
whether " The Two Noble Kinſmen," " Titus Andronicus," " Pericles," and the firſt and ſecond parts of
" Henry VI." were canonical or apocryphal; what
ſhould be the received text—the folio of 1623 or that
of 1632—and what the authority of the quartos; he
would pronounce upon the validity of the claims of
various readings, and winnow the whole crop of com-
mentators, from Malone, Farmer, Theobald, Steevens,
and Johnſon, down to Collier, Dyce, and the Cambridge
editors. And ſo at length the republic of letters might
repoſe upon infallible authority, and not be, as it now
is, a prey to unhappy diviſions, and diſtracted by the
uncertain ſound emitted by its contending teachers.

But to return from my digreſſion.

Having ſeen poor little Stornaway made comfortable
in a looſe box, to reſt after his long journey, and left
Smoker to keep him company, I walked out to take a
general ſurvey of the town. The High Street I have
already deſcribed. Henley Street, which branches off
from it at the market-place, is built of mean houſes,
and has nothing remarkable about it but Shakeſpere's
birthplace, of which I ſhall ſpeak preſently. Chapel
Street, where New Place once ſtood, has much more
character. But everybody ſeems to have conſpired to

deface this town. The Town Hall is an ugly modern
building, and the Guild Chapel of the Holy Crofs is in
the debafed ftyle of the reign of Henry VII., when Sir
Hugh Clopton built it on the ruins of an older edifice,
the chancel of which ftill bears evidence to its fuperior
beauty. The clumfy tower is feen to the left in the
photograph of the Grammar School. In the chapel
is the tomb of Sir Hugh, on which is the following
infcription : "He built ye ftone bridge over Avon, with
ye caufey at ye Weft End; further manifefting his
piety to God and love to this place of his nativity (as
ye centurion in ye Gofpel did to ye Jewifh Nation and
Religion by building them a fynagogue), for at his fole
charge this beautiful chappell of ye Holy Trinity was
rebuilt, temp. H. VII., and ye crofs ifle of ye Parifh
Church." Inftead of, perhaps, a beautiful Early Englifh or Decorated building, we have one of clumfy
proportions and debafed ornamentation. Such as it is,
however, it has been further debafed by the church-
wardens or common-councillors of the eighteenth
century. Profeffor Willis has well obferved, that when-
ever a church wanted rebuilding or decoration in the
middle ages, fome Saint, or Saint's relics, were fure
providentially to turn up in the neighbourhood. The
clergy immediately enfhrined them, the people flocked
to pay their devotions, and the church was renovated

by means of their pious offerings. Surely the votaries
of Shakespere ought to offer for the restoration of a
shrine whose shadow fell upon his house, upon which
he must have looked from his windows, and where he
probably used often to kneel. Little besides the clearing
away of a quantity of ugly cumbrous church furniture
would be enough to restore it to nearly the same
appearance as it bore when Shakespere knew it. It
would now be impossible, even if such a proceeding
were sanctioned by public opinion, to restore the beautiful frescoes discovered in 1804, when the chapel was
repaired. The chief subject was the " Invention of
the Holy Cross," to which the chapel was dedicated;
but that which probably brought the swiftest ruin
upon the whole was the " Martyrdom of Thomas-a-
Beckett," to whose memory Henry VIII. bore special
enmity, because the ground of the " blissful martyr's "
canonization was his resistance to the power of the
crown. His name is carefully erased from all missals
and other service-books used in Henry's reign. The
frescoes were therefore probably defaced by the Refor-
mers even before they were finally destroyed in 1804.
They were, however, copied, and have been published.

Passing on from the Guild Chapel, we have the
whole range of buildings containing the Grammar
School and Guildhall, and, near the parish church, a

nice-looking old houfe, built on the fite of the old college for priefts, which was pulled down in 1799.

The parifh church is a very fine fpecimen of Perpendicular, built on the banks of the Avon, and furrounded by trees. I fhall fpeak of it more at length in connection with Shakefpere's grave and monument. The bridge, the chapel, the church, the Poet's birthplace in Henley Street, and the old houfe in Chapel Street, of which Mr. Edwards has taken an excellent photograph, are the only vifible remains of the period when Shakefpere lived here. They may ferve to give us fome idea of how Stratford looked in his time.

In the firft place, then, the ftreets were not, as now, compofed of rows of uninterefting brick cottages. The dwelling-houfes were probably detached, and furrounded by yards and gardens, like John Shakefpere's, in Henley Street. Of the ftyle of the fhop-fronts, the fhop of Mr. Williams, breeches-maker, glover, &c. (fee photograph), will give us an idea; and a ftreet of fuch fronts, with the fhape, and height, and ornamentation of each varied indefinitely, muft have been very beautiful. There, on the top of the hill upon which the town ftands, was the old market crofs, a picturefque Gothic ftructure, round which the chapmen affembled, and fhowed their merchandife, and perhaps fome *Autolycus* fung:—

" Will you buy any tape,
  Or lace for your cape,
My dainty duck, my dear-a ;
  Any ſilk, any thread,
  Any toys for your head,
Of the new'ſt and fin'ſt, fin'ſt wear-a ;
  Come to the pedlar,
  Money's a meddler
That doth alter all men's wear-a."

Here, near the church, was the old college for prieſts, appropriated by Maſter John à Combe as a dwelling-houſe on the diſſolution of the religious houſes, but ſtill retaining its ſtately eccleſiaſtical character. The church and chapel were ſhorn, indeed, of their former glories, and a coat of whitewaſh had perhaps been laid on the walls to deface any traces of colour or painting; but the carved benches or chairs, the rood-ſcreen, and the ſtained glaſs probably yet remained, and the galleries and pews were as yet in the womb of time. Chapel Street was adorned and dignified by New Place, a fine old manſion built by the magnificent Sir Hugh Clopton. In ſuch a town, built on a riſing ground on the banks of the Avon, cloſe to the parks of Fulbrooke and Charlecote and the Foreſt of Arden, the Poet of Nature might well have been proud to have been born, and glad to dwell amongſt his own people.

CHAPTER III.

I HAD now got fo far as this in my inveftigation:—
The place of Shakefpere's birth—where he fpent his
youth, and to which he retired the moment he had
acquired a competence—was in his time, notwithftanding its prefent dreary appearance, a town embellifhed
by many ftately and beautiful buildings, the refidence
of wealthy burghers and of a large body of clergy,
at that time the moft learned and cultivated clafs of
fociety. It was moreover built on the banks of a
lovely river, furrounded by rural villages, parks, and
foreft tracts—fuch a country, in fhort, as would feize
upon the fancy of a poet, and mark his imagination
with the imprefs of its own character. For though
the poet's fancy be, in one fenfe, independent of outward things, and

> " Doth glance from heaven to earth, and earth to heaven,
> And as imagination bodies forth
> The forms of things unknown, the poet's pen
> Turns them to fhapes, and gives to airy nothing
> A local habitation and a name,"

yet if, as Locke afferts, the mind be a fheet of white paper till written upon by the fenfes, the original fimple ideas from which the complex images of poetry are formed muft have had their origin in outward things, however independent of them they may afterwards become. And that Shakefpere's young imagination fed upon the fcenes in which his youth was fpent is plain, both from the fact that he never loft fight of the grand object of returning to live in his native town, and from the whole character of his writings. None of his contemporaries has drawn fo directly and fo largely from Englifh rural life as he, and the ftyle of fcenery upon which he delights to dwell, as defcribed, for inftance, in the words of *Titania*—

> " And never, fince the middle fummer's fpring,
> Met we on hill, in dale, foreft, or mead,
> By pavèd fountain, or by rufhy brook "—

is juft that of the neighbourhood of Stratford. Greene and Peele have fome pretty country fcenes, but they want the touches of nature, the elegance, the lightnefs of the mafter. In thefe refpects no one approaches him but Chaucer, whofe merits are unhappily buried for the generality in his obfolete language, and whofe occafional groffnefs condemns his poems to clofe prifon. To quote inftances of Shakefpere's power of depicting Englifh country fcenes and people would be to tranfcribe a great part of his plays. But to take an inſtance : " As You Like It " is ſaid to be more generally read than any other of his works; and this is owing, I think, to the hold which the idea of life in the Foreſt of Arden has on the reader, who finds in the ſhepherds and ſhepherdeſſes, not the Arcadian article, but the real Engliſh one. And where did Shakeſpere get his Foreſt of Arden ? Not, we may be ſure, in Flanders, but in the foreſt tract of Warwickſhire. Of Engliſh middle claſs ſociety in a country town, where ſhall we find a more life-like or genial picture than in " The Merry Wives of Windſor ? " *Page, Ford,* and their wives, *Sir Hugh Evans,* and the hoſt of the " Garter " were doubtleſs drawn from the ſubſtantial glovers and wool-ſtaplers, innkeepers and parſons, of Stratford and the neighbourhood. Of the home of a wealthy juſtice of the peace in a remote county *Shallow's* houſe and ſurroundings is the trueſt and moſt humorous concep-tion that ever was penned.

But to gather from the place all the inſight which it can yield, we muſt take into account eſpecially the poſition which the Poet held there in his youth. The impreſſion made upon the mind, of the young eſpecially, by outward objects, depends much upon the ſtanding-point from which it views them. A peer and a coſtermonger ſhall both inhabit London, but yet their several conceptions of the place shall differ as widely as if one lived in Timbuctoo and the other in Siberia.

The family of Shakespere, which had been long settled in Warwickshire, appears never to have risen above the rank of the yeomanry. The Poet's father, John Shakespere, was the son of Richard Shakespere, a farmer of Snitterfield, not far from Stratford, and resided in the house in Henley Street which tradition assigns as the place of the Poet's birth. In an entry in the register of the Bailiff's Court of that town, dated 1556, stating that he was sued by Thomas Siche of Arscotte in Wiltshire for £8, he is described as "Johannes Shakespere de Stretford in Comitatu Warici, *Glover.*" It appears that he also farmed land, or at least sold corn and timber, for in the same year he sued Henry Fyld for eighteen quarters of barley, which the latter unjustly detained. In 1564 the corporation of Stratford paid him 4*s.* for a piece of timber. In the same year—the year of his celebrated son's birth —he contributed towards the relief of the poor when the plague was raging in the town. He occupied a farm of fourteen acres at Ington Meadow, or Ingon —*Ing* means " meadow," as in Ingatestone, called in Latin, *Pratum apud petram*—and in 1575 he purchased two freehold houses in Henley Street. One of these he had before occupied as tenant—that, namely, in which

William Shakefpere was in all probability born. In a
deed dated 1579 he is defcribed as a yeoman, and his
name is found in a roll of the gentlemen and freeholders
of Barlifh hundred, in which Stratford is fituated, bearing date 1580. In a deed dated 1596 he is again
defcribed as a yeoman. In 1586 the copyhold of a
houfe in Henley Street was affigned to him.

We have feen that in one document he is ftyled
" glover," and that from others it appears that he
farmed land. Aubrey fays he was a butcher, and
Rowe, that he was a confiderable dealer in wool. But
all thefe are callings which might very poffibly be exercifed by one and the fame perfon. Even at the prefent
day, when the principle of the divifion of labour is
much more rigidly carried out than formerly, we often
fee farmers combining with their principal callings thofe
of butchers, general dealers, timber-merchants, charcoal-
burners, horfe-dealers, corn-factors, auctioneers, valuers,
or fuch like country trades. In thofe times it was ftill
more likely that a man of active mind and of fome
claim to gentility fhould be impatient of the fmall
profits of farming, and fhould try fome fhort cut to
wealth by fpeculating in any bufinefs with which circumftances might have made him acquainted.

At any rate he muft have been a man of fome
ftanding and influence in his native town, for in 1557

he was appointed an ale-tafter and a burgefs; in 1558 and 1559 he ferved as conftable—an office generally held by refpectable farmers or tradefmen; in 1561 he was appointed afferor—an officer defined by Cowel, " Such as are appointed in court-leets, &c., upon oath, to mulct fuch as have committed faults arbitrarily punifhable, and have no exprefs penalty fet down by ftatute." He was elected one of the chamberlains in 1561; an alderman in 1565; high bailiff in 1568; and on September 5, 1571, he was again elected alderman for the enfuing year. From fome of the documents from which thefe facts are recorded, it has been argued that John Shakefpere could not write his name, for he has made his mark at the foot of feveral of them. At that time the inability to write was not confidered fo difgraceful as it would now be. But that John Shake-fpere figned his mark and not his name is by no means decifive of the fact that he could not write. I think it is Dr. Maitland who obferves, in his book on the middle ages, that it was then confidered a mark of dignity to have your name written by a clerk, and merely to acknowledge the act by making a crofs or other mark oppofite it.

It has often been obferved that men of genius favour —to ufe a provincial, but, I think, alfo a Shakefperian word—their mother, rather than their father; a prin-

ciple acted upon by the Arabs, who are faid to count
the pedigrees of their horfes through the dams, and
not the fires. It may be fo in the cafe of men, but the
fact, if it be one, may alfo be due to the early education imparted by mothers to their children. Education begins, in fact, at the mother's knee; and the
bent given to the youthful mind from infancy to eight
or nine years old, during the long hours fpent at home
while the father is at his work, is probably difcernible
for ever after. Was it fo in the cafe of Shakefpere?
We cannot tell, indeed, for certain; but ftill the mind,
in dealing with the myfterious problem of his genius,
clings to anything in the fhape of even a probability.
When we read "Hamlet," "The Moor of Venice,"
"The Merchant of Venice," "As You Like It," "Much-
Ado About Nothing," "Lear," "Cymbeline," or "Romeo and Juliet," we are amazed at the variety of character difplayed in *Ophelia, Defdemona, Portia, Rofalind,
Celia, Hermione, Beatrice, Cordelia, Imogen,* and *Juliet;*
but in each we recognife fundamental truth to the
higheft type of woman's nature. How did he obtain
the moral infight and elevation neceffary as a foundation on which to raife thefe various fuperftructures?
Where did he, a wild young man, fpending his youth
among the young farmers and tradefmen of Stratford,
and his manhood about the London theatres, acquire

that reverence for women which enabled him to com-
bine in his female characters the wildest passion with
the moft exquisite purity? Clever sons have often had
foolish mothers; but if any man has a tender refpect for
women and a deep appreciation of female excellence,
I think it will be found that he has acquired thefe
qualities from the early lessons of maternal love. I
am willing, therefore, to fancy that Shakespere obtained his faculty of forming his high ideal of female
character from the early impressions left upon his
mind by his mother.

Her very name, Mary Arden, is fuggeftive. The
painters have taken care that the firft bearer of the
name of Mary shall prefent to our minds all that is
pureft, nobleft, moft graceful, and womanly in maid,
wife, and mother. The fimple country folk give her
name to the moft wholefome, the fweeteft, and the
prettieft herbs and flowers that grow in their gardens
and hedges—the rofemary, the marygold, the lady's
flipper, the maiden-hair, the lady's fingers, and other
fuch like. Arden means a foreft, and is applied, by way
of excellence, to the foreft country in Warwickshire,
and that on the borders of France and Flanders, the
fcene of " As You Like It " and " Quentin Durward."

Of Mary Arden, indeed, no perfonal record remains,
but we know this at leaft, that she was of an old and

wealthy Warwickfhire family, fome members of which had done good fervice to Henry VII. Her father was Robert Arden, a gentleman of Wilmecote, in the pa-rifhes of Stratford-upon-Avon and Afton, from whom fhe inherited the eftate of Afhbies, confifting of about fifty-four acres, two tenements in Snitterfield, a fhare in other lands at Wilmecote, befides a fmall fum of money. The family derived its name from the foreft diftrict of Arden, whence the Poet, no doubt, took his ideal of the Arden whofe trees Orlando " marred with writing love-fongs in their barks." That the heirefs of Wilmecote inherited fome gentle qualities from her gentle anceftry is poffible ; and its probability will not be gainfayed by thofe who know what a difference the fact of a pointer being fhot over or left untrained, makes in the fteadinefs of its offspring. The fagacity acquired by affociation with man's fuperior intelligence is tranfmitted from generation to generation in the lower animals ; and that in man the qualities of mind foftered by the habitual felf-refpect, intellectual activity, and purfuit of noble aims, which, as a general rule, are found only amongft thofe who are exempt from a dependence upon bodily toil, fhould alfo defcend with the blood, is not improbable ; but that her father's eafy circumftances fecured to Mary Arden the un-queftionable benefits of a good education, there can

be no reafonable doubt. And fo Shakefpere, perhaps, might add one more inftance to confirm the fuppofed rule that the genius of great men defcends to them from their mothers' qualities or training. He was born, in fact, upon the outfkirts of gentility, and was excluded from the tempting inner circle by poverty rather than by birth.

I had now to vifit the actual houfe—nay, the very room—in which he probably firft faw the light.

In this houfe refided his father, John Shakefpere, probably as a tenant, in 1552. In 1556 he purchafed the freehold, and was refident there in 1590. The baptifm of his third child, William, is regiftered in the parifh church, under the date of April 26, 1564; and therefore it feems almoft certain that the Poet was born in this houfe, his parents' ufual refidence, in accordance with the uninterrupted tradition of the place.

Mr. Edwards, with camera more potent than the perfpective glafs of Friar Bacon, or the wand with which *Profpero* commanded the fervices of his "trickfy *Ariel*," has compelled the bleffed Sun himfelf to paint us four pictures of this interefting relic. It is built of timber, with the interftices filled in with what is called "wattle and dab," and probably refembled moft other houfes of its clafs in the old town of

Stratford; but I was not prepared to fee it look fo fmug and new. Many of the old timbers remain, and the houfe is, indeed, fubftantially the fame houfe as it was; but new timbers have been inferted where the old were decayed, everything has been fcraped and polifhed up, and the place looks as if it had been "reftored," a word to ftrike terror to the heart of an antiquary, not to fpeak of a man of tafte. The propenfity to ftain, and polifh, and varnifh, and fub-ftitute new work for old unneceffarily, is much to be deprecated. Perhaps the committee, who hold the property in truft for the nation, could not avoid giving to Shakefpere's birthplace its prefent holiday appear-ance; but how often is the artiftic eye offended by feeing a fine old building vulgarifed by reftorers! There is an ancient log-church at Grinftead, near Chipping Ongar, in this county, which is enough to make one tear one's hair. The trunks of the trees of which it is built, and which were all riven and white with age, have been fcraped, and ftained, and varnifhed; old ftone-work has been replaced by the moft neatly-pointed brick; windows filled with the weather-ftained green glafs of centuries ago, have been re-glazed in the neweft fafhion; an enormous and very conceited-looking eagle ftands in the middle of the nave, and the whole place is encumbered with berlin-wool im-

pertinences. The worſt of it is, that the perpetrators of ſuch enormities are generally ſuch worthy, well-meaning people, that one is afraid to ſuggeſt a doubt as to their diſcretion, for fear of damping their zeal. Perhaps a few years' expoſure to the weather may tone down the " neat" look of the houſe in Henley Street.

The firſt room I entered was in that part of the building which had been a butcher's ſhop, and which, I believe, was the reſidence of John Shakeſpere. It ſeemed to be a ſort of hall, or outer kitchen, paved with unſhapely flags. The great old fire-place is ſupported by immenſe ſtone jambs, and the ceiling by a ponderous beam. Opening out of this is a better room, probably the keeping-room, or, as it is called in Yorkſhire, the " houſe-place." This, too, is paved with flags, and ſupported by beams. The fire-place is maſſive, and under its projecting jambs are coſy chimney-corners, where, doubtleſs, young Shakeſpere, ſeated on a ſettle, many a time conned his leſſons of a winter's evening, or read in Holinſhed, or roaſted crabs for the lambs'-wool, or, perhaps, dried himſelf after one of his raids upon a neighbouring park or warren. Beyond this are two ſmaller rooms, which were probably bed-chambers; and beyond them, again, ſome more rooms, which, there ſeems every reaſon to believe, formed part of the other adjoining houfe, and which are not fhown. Upftairs is the bed-chamber in which tradition afferts the great Poet to have been born; and tradition is probably right, for it is the beft chamber in the houfe, and therefore probably appropriated to the miftrefs on fuch an occafion. The large window in the firft photograph belongs to it, and the fecond places the interior before the reader's eyes as it exifts; and if he cannot actually be prefent at Stratford on the 23rd of April next, he can fee all that the veritable pilgrims will fee without ftirring out of his arm-chair. Every fquare inch of the walls is covered with the names of vifitors, attefting the univerfal homage paid to the mighty genius who reflects his fame upon the unconfcious ftone and mafonry. The jambs of the chimney have been appropriated by the modern actors and actreffes, and amongft their names may ftill be read that of Edmund Kean. Sir Walter Scott has infcribed his in indelible characters with a diamond on a pane of glafs in the large window.

In another room on the fame floor is fhown a portrait, much refembling the buft in the church, and faid to have been preferved for many years in the family of Mr. William Oakes Hunt, town-clerk of Stratford, by whom it has been prefented to the public. It is very like the monument in the church.

After looking at thefe things for a while, and lingering over them with a fort of vague feeling that they ought to tell fomething of him to whom they were once familiar—the feeling, I fuppofe which made men brave every danger to vifit Jerufalem, and which ftill impels them to traverfe the defert that they may tread the ftreets of Mecca—I paffed out by a back-door into the garden, which is nicely laid out with gravel-walks, and in the middle of which may be feen fome carved ftones taken from the ruins of New Place. This fupplied Mr. Edwards with another view of the houfe.

There was a fcheme, I think, fuggefted of planting this garden exclufively with plants mentioned in Shake-fpere's works, but it was abandoned. Perhaps it would be impoffible to carry the idea out thoroughly; but I would certainly plead for a place for poor *Ophelia's* "rofemary, that's for remembrance," and "panfies, that's for thought;" her fennel and her columbines, and "herb-o'-grace o' Sundays." I would have here—

"Daifies pied, and violets blue,
And lady's fmocks all filver white,
And cuckoo-buds of yellow hue;"

and *Titania's* "mufk-rofes" fhould be there too—not forgetting the "little weftern flower," which maidens call " Love in Idlenefs ;" and fweet *Perdita's*

> " —————Daffodils,
> That come before the fwallow dares, and take
> The winds of March with beauty ; violets, dim,
> But fweeter than the lids of Juno's eyes,
> Or Cytherea's breath ; pale primrofes,
> That die unmarried, ere they can behold
> Bright Phœbus in his ftrength : a malady
> Moft incident to maids ; bold oxlips, and
> The crown-imperial ; lilies of all kinds,
> The flower-de-luce being one."

Thefe gardens are intended for the delectation of the public, and it would certainly contribute to the intereft and amufement of vifitors if, as they walked, they could read on labels the many charming paffages in which the great Poet, like One ftill greater, fhowed his love of nature by taking fimilitudes and pointing morals from " the lilies of the field."

In this houfe, then, which is that of a refpectable yeoman, was William Shakefpere born, fome few days before the 26th of April, 1564, the date of his bap-tifm. The period allowed to elapfe between his birth and baptifm was, probably, not more than eight days ; becaufe the analogy between the Jewifh rite and the Chriftian facrament was then maintained ; and a fuper-ftition prevailed, that if the time were deferred longer, the infant might be carried off by the fairies, and an ouf fubftituted in its place. Here, at any rate, his

Shakspere's House from the Garden.

(THE GARDEN SEAT A CARVED STONE REMOVED FROM NEW PLACE)

boyhood and youth were fpent, and he paffed through
the ages defcribed by himfelf:—

> " At firft the infant,
> Mewling and puking in the nurfe's arms ;
> Then the whining fchoolboy, with his fatchel,
> With fhining morning face, creeping like fnail,
> Unwillingly to fchool ; and then the lover,
> Sighing like furnace, with a woful ballad
> Made to his miftrefs' eyebrow."

Before difmiffing the fubject of the houfe in Henley
Street, it may be well to record the viciffitudes through
which it has paffed.   John Shakefpere, the Poet's
father, appears to have lived in a freehold houfe in
Henley Street, as tenant, in the year 1552.   In 1574,
he purchafed from Edmund Hall, and Emma his wife,
for forty pounds, the houfes, defcribed as " two meffuages, two gardens, and two orchards, with their appurtenances ;" and one of thefe was, probably, that
which he already occupied as tenant.   On the death
of John Shakefpere, thefe houfes defcended to his eldeft
fon, William ; and here, probably, the Poet's wife and
family lived while he was working for them in
London. The houfes continued to belong to him after
he had purchafed New Place, and he bequeathed " the
two meffuages, or tenements, with the appurtenance,
fituate, &c., in Henley Street, within the borough of
Stratford," to his daughter, Sufanna Hall, from whom

they defcended to her daughter, Elizabeth, married, firft, to Thomas Nafh, and, fecondly, to Sir William Barnard. Lady Barnard bequeathed the property, defcribed in her will as " the inn, called the ' Maidenhead,' and the adjoining houfe and barn," to Thomas and George Hart, the grandchildren of Shakefpere's fifter Joan, in the poffeffion of whofe defcendants they remained till the beginning of this century. The name of the inn was, however, changed from the " Maidenhead," to the " White Lion," and the adjoining houfe was ufed as a butcher's fhop. In this ftate they continued, the property of private perfons; and, at one time, there was a rumour that fome American—Barnum, perhaps —was about to buy them, and tranfport them bodily, like the Holy Houfe of Loretto, to Bofton. This act of facrilege was prevented by the appointment of a committee of gentlemen, amongft the reft, Lord Carlifle, who collected fubfcriptions, and bought them for the nation. Rightly deeming that the prefervation of the houfe was the firft object, they pulled down the adjoining tenements to prevent the danger of fire, repaired the houfe where it was decayed, and laid out the wafte ground in gardens. In 1854, Mr. John Shakefpere, of Afhby-de-la-Zouche, left by will a fum of £2,000, to be employed in reftoring the houfe, efta-blifhing a mufeum of Shakefperian relics, and paying a curator; but the bequeſt was held by the Court of Chancery to be bad for its indefinitenefs, and contrary to the proviſions of the Statute of Mortmain. Sufficient funds were, however, obtained, by ſubſcription, to put the premiſes into their preſent very creditable ſtate of repair; and the Shakeſperian pilgrims who viſit the place next ſpring will, no doubt, make up any deficiency.

CHAPTER IV.

The next object of interest was the Grammar School, founded in the reign of Edward VI., by Thomas Jolepe. The prefent buildings, which comprife the guildhall and the fchoolroom, are in Chapel Street, and form part of a long row, the upper ftory of which projects over the lower, after the manner of ancient dwellings. The reader may fee it in Mr. Edwards's photograph, with the tower of the Guild Chapel in the background. It was during the play-hour that I vifited it, and the head-mafter very kindly fhowed me over the place. You afcend a flight of ftairs to reach the fchoolroom, which has much the fame appearance as other rooms devoted to a like purpofe. The ceiling has lately been removed and the oak roof revealed, which, with the aid of the latticed windows, gives the room an ancient and venerable appearance, fuch as it bore when Shakefpere learned his accidence here.

Much ftrefs has been laid upon a fuppofition that

Shakefpere was taught in "a fchool i' the church;" and indeed there is evidence that at one time the fchool was held in the Guild Chapel. But the mode of education was the fame whether it were given in the church or in a feparate building. A chantry prieft, or the parifh prieft himfelf, was often the fchoolmafter, and held the fchool in the foler over the church porch, and the foundation of the education he gave was grammar—the grammar of the Latin language as being the moft fcientific and accurate. At that time fchoolmafters were not fo foolifh as to teach Latin grammar and Englifh grammar feparately, as if they were two diftinct branches of knowledge. Latin was the medium for teaching grammar in general, and, therefore, we may be fure that through it Shakefpere learned the elements of the fcience of language, in which he proved fo great a mafter.

In the fixteenth century Greek was only beginning to be generally ftudied. Erafmus, Rabelais, Sir Thomas More, and Dean Collet had up-hill work in recommending the ftudy, and were vehemently oppofed by the confervatives in the old feats of learning. In fome of the great grammar fchools it was introduced in the reign of Edward VI., as, for inftance, at Chrift's Hofpital, where the moft advanced ftudents are ftill called Grecians. Chapman, who was fenior to Shakefpere, tranflated

Homer, though his fcholarfhip was certainly not great, as may be feen by his notes; and Marlowe, Greene, and Peele, the " Univerfity pens," as they were called, knew enough of it perhaps to fwear by. But even this fmall amount of Greek, Shakefpere had no means of acquiring. He could not have remained at the Stratford grammar fchool long enough to become anything like a fcholar; but without becoming fo familiar even with Latin as to read it for pleafure, or acquiring a critical knowledge of Latin authors, he certainly learned the fcience of language to fuch good purpofe that his power of wielding words is unrivalled. And this is, after all, the beft fruit of fcholarfhip.

It is related fomewhere that Wilkie, feeing a grotefque face, and not having the materials of his art by him, drew it on his thumb-nail, and introduced it in one of his pictures; and Shakefpere, no doubt, like a true artift, loft no opportunity of obferving any old character he came acrofs and embodying it in his plays. Now amongft the names of the fchoolmafters who wielded the ferule at Stratford, I think we may find the probable prototype of a very amufing perfonage in the " Merry Wives of Windfor." In 1570, when Shakefpere was fix years old, the fchoolmafter was Walter Roche. In 1572, when he was eight years old, Thomas Hunt, curate of Shottery, came into

power; and in 1580 Thomas Jenkins was inftalled.
Shakefpere was then fixteen, an age at which boys are
very keen to detect the weakneffes of their mafters.
In the "Merry Wives of Windfor" he pays off Sir
Thomas Lucy; may he not alfo have drawn his quon-
dam pedagogue in the admirable fcene where *Sir
Hugh Evans* puts *William Page* through his parts of
fpeech? Thomas Jenkins is obvioufly the name of a
Welfhman, for which the Poet probably fubftituted
the equally Welfh combination of names, Hugh Evans.
At fixteen, Shakefpere had either left, or was about
to leave, fchool, and therefore we can hardly fuppofe
"William" to have been himfelf; but he may have
remained for a time after he had finifhed his own
ftudies to affift Jenkins—and this, by the way, would
account for the tradition that he was at one time a
fchoolmafter—when he would have had abundant
opportunities of obferving fuch fcenes as the following. We might, therefore, perhaps, read "Thomas
Jenkins" for "Hugh Evans" in this paffage :—

Mrs. Page. How now, Sir Hugh? no fchool to-day?

Evans. No; Mafter Slender is let the boys leave to play.

Quickly. Bleffings of his heart!

Mrs. Page. Sir Hugh, my hufband fays my fon profits nothing in the
world at his book; I pray you, afk him fome queftions in his accidence.

Evans. Come hither, William; hold up your head, come.

Mrs. Page. Come on, firrah : hold up your head; anfwer your mafter,
be not afraid.

Evans. William, how many numbers is in nouns?

William. Two.

Quickly. Truly, I thought there had been one number more; becaufe they fay od's nouns.

Evans. Peace your tattlings. What is *fair*, William?

William. *Pulcher.*

Quickly. Polecats! there are fairer things than polecats, fure.

Evans. You are a very fimplicity 'oman; I pray you, peace. What is *lapis*, William?

William. A ftone.

Evans. And what is a ftone, William?

William. A pebble.

Evans. No, it is *lapis;* I pray you remember in your prain.

William. Lapis.

Evans. That is a good William. What is he, William, that doth lend articles?

William. Articles are borrowed of the pronoun; and be thus declined, *Singulariter, nominativo, hic, hæc, hoc.*

Evans. Nominativo, hig, hag, hog;—I pray you mark: *genitivo, hujus.* Well, what is your *accusative case?*

William. Accusativo, hunc.

Evans. I pray you, have your remembrance, child; *Accusativo, hung, hang, hog.*

Quickly. Hang hog is Latin for bacon, I warrant you.

Evans. Leave your prabbles, 'oman. What is the focative case, William?

William. O—vocativo O.

Evans. Remember, William, focative is, *caret.*

Quickly. And that's a good root.

If poor William Shakefpere learned his accidence in this ftyle, it is no wonder that he had " fmall Latin ;" and Farmer has clearly fhown that the tradition of his lack of fcholarfhip, embodied even in the encomiums of his contemporaries, is probably true. But perhaps Thomas Hunt, the curate of Shottery, was a better fcholar than Thomas Jenkins.

The grammar fchool is alfo probably the parent of the comical fcene in " Love's Labour Loft," where _Sir Nathaniel_—called " Sir " becaufe a Mafter of Arts—and _Holofernes_, the fchoolmafter or pedant, fhow off their learning before _Goodman Dull_; but whether _Holofernes_ were intended to reprefent either William Roche or Thomas Hunt we have no means even to form a conjecture.

Nathaniel. Very reverend fport, truly; and done in the teftimony of a good confcience.

Holofernes. The deer was, as you know, _fanguis_,—in blood; ripe as a pomewater, who now hangeth like a jewel in the ear of _cœlo_—the fky, the welkin, the heaven; and anon falleth like a crab, on the face of _terra_—the foil, the land, the earth.

Nathaniel. Truly, Mafter Holofernes, the epithets are fweetly varied, like a fcholar at the leaft; but, fir, I affure you, it was a buck of the firft head.

Holofernes. Sir Nathaniel, _haud credo._

Dull. 'Twas not a _haud credo_; 'twas a pricket.

Holofernes. Moft barbarous intimation! yet a kind of infinuation as it were, _in via_, in way, of explication; _facere_, as it were, replication; or, rather, _oftentare_, to fhow, as it were, his inclination, after his undreffed, unpolifhed, uneducated, unpruned, untrained, or rather unlettered, or, rathereft, unconformed fafhion—to infert again my _haud credo_ for a deer.

Dull. I faid the deer was not a _haud credo_; 'twas a pricket.

Holofernes. Twice fod fimplicity, _bis coctus!_—O thou monfter igno-rance, how deformed doft thou look!

Nathaniel. Sir, he hath never fed of the dainties that are bred in a book: he doth not eat paper, as it were; he hath not drunk ink: his intellect is not replenished; he is only an animal, only fensible in the duller parts.

It is not unlikely that Shakefpere, in this excellent caricature of a fcholar, may have intended to retaliate upon Ben Jonfon and his other more learned friends for their reflections upon his "fmall Latin." The whole fcene is an example of the euphuifm brought into fafhion by Lilly—the far-fetched and fantaftic ftyle which has defcended to the fecond-rate writers in newfpapers. A man who, like Shakefpere, has fed upon the banquet that Nature provided for him, is apt to be a little impatient of thofe who have, " as it were, eaten paper and drunk ink," juft as Lord Bacon told his friend, Sir Thomas Bodley, that he was going to write a treatife againft great libraries.

CHAPTER V.

FROM the grammar fchool in Chapel Street I returned to Henley Street, and from thence, by a footpath acrofs the fields and over ftiles, to the little village of Shottery. Many a time had Shakefpere trodden this very path when he had attained the lover ftage of life, " fighing like a furnace, with a woful ballad made to his miftrefs' eyebrow." Here, perhaps, when the fighs became too deep, he may have cheered himfelf with—

> " Jog on, jog on, the footpath way,
> And merrily hent the ftile-a;
> Your merry heart goes all the day,
> Your fad one tires in a mile-a."

The village is a ftraggling one, and the cottages are picturefque though poor. At the bottom of the village to the left of a pretty country lane, ftands the cottage to which tradition points as having been the refidence of Anne Hathaway, who afterwards became the Poet's wife. The reader will at once fee its character from Mr. Edwards's charming little photograph.

It was once obvioufly a fubftantial farm-houfe, much fuperior to that of John Shakefpere in Henley Street, though, like it, built of wooden frames filled in with wattle and dab on foundations of ftone. In modern times brick has been in fome places fubftituted where the ftone has become decayed. The roof is thatched, I think with reed. It is now divided into two cottages, and Mrs. Baker, a pleafing refpectable-looking woman, who believes herfelf to be related to the Hathaways, lives in a portion of it. She is proud of her connection with the Poet—an honour which fhe appreciates the more, perhaps, as it brings her in many a fhilling from the pilgrims who flock to fee the houfe. She willingly fhows the infide of her dwelling, and feveral pieces of old furniture which, as fhe avers, have defcended to her from her anceftors. If fo, and there is no reafon to doubt the fact, they may very poffibly have been ufed by young Shakefpere when he was courting his future wife.

A flight of fteps leads into a large keeping room or hall, where under the great old chimney may have fat Shakefpere and his love, in the days of his extreme youth when Love is ftone blind. In a family Bible Mrs. Baker fhows the following pedigree, in which fhe

traces her defcent from the Hathaways, who have continued to refide in the houfe ever fince the fixteenth century.

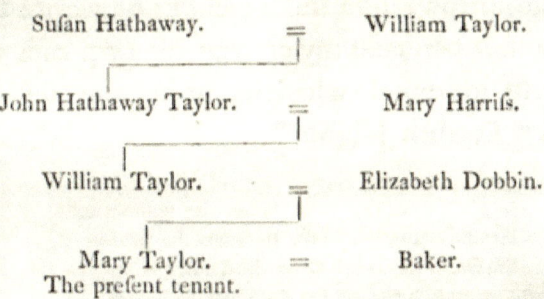

Sufan Hathaway. = William Taylor.

John Hathaway Taylor. = Mary Harrifs.

William Taylor. = Elizabeth Dobbin.

Mary Taylor. = Baker.
The prefent tenant.

Upftairs is a bed-chamber, where Mrs. Baker fhows an old oak bed and a pair of very beautifully worked fheets and pillow-cafes. She fays fhe inherited them from her father, and that they have been in the family from time immemorial, and ufed on ftate occafions, fuch as marriages, births, and deaths. They are marked " Elizabeth Hathaway," but whether the character of the work be ancient or modern I am not fuch an adept in needlework as to determine. About the houfe are feveral old oak chefts, chairs, and fettles, but none, I fhould imagine, older than the feventeenth century.

Much has been written refpecting Shakefpere's marriage, and perhaps a good deal of it rafhly. The circum- ftances are not, affuredly, very fatisfactory. In the firft place he was under nineteen when he married, and

Anne Hathaway was fix and twenty. And though he
was not a man to make literary capital out of his
domeftic relations, or to whine in public over his re-
grets and forrows, like the fnivelling hypocrite Greene,
yet I cannot perfuade myfelf that his own cafe was not
prefent to his mind when he wrote the well-known
lines in "Twelfth Night:"—

> " Let the woman take
> An elder than herfelf; fo wears fhe to him;
> So fways the level in her hufband's heart;
> For, boy, however we do praife ourfelves,
> Our fancies are more giddy and infirm,
> More longing, wavering, fooner loft and worn
> Than women's are.
> Then let thy love be younger than thyfelf,
> Or thy affection cannot hold the bent."

Anne Hathaway was the daughter of one Richard
Hathaway, a fmall farmer. The marriage bond and
licenfe were difcovered in the Confiftorial Court at
Worcefter in the year 1836, by Sir Robert Phillipps.
They are dated November 28, 1582, and are marked
with croffes. One of the feals has the initials "R. H.,"
fuppofed to be thofe of the bride's father, Richard
Hathaway. There is no record of the marriage in
Stratford church; it therefore muft have been folem-
nifed in the church of fome neighbouring village, where
the regifters have not been preferved, or perhaps in a

private houfe. The regifter of Stratford bears witnefs, however, to the birth of the firft-born of William Shakefpere and Anne Hathaway, in May, 1583.

From thefe ugly facts, Mr. de Quincy, in his article on Shakefpere, in the " Encyclopædia Britannica," has perhaps drawn unwarrantable conclufions. The agreement to live as man and wife is held, I believe, by the canon law to conftitute marriage. Manzoni's " I Promeffi Spofi" is founded upon this principle, which ftill prevails even in Proteftant Scotland, while the law of the country follows that of Rome in many of its principles and forms. The religious ceremony was held to be merely a folemn ratification of a contract already complete, and to be in nowife effential to its perfection. Hence, the marriage of heathens has always been held good, and not to be repeated on the parties becoming Chriftians. Every nation has, of courfe, a right to require certain forms to be gone through in order to prevent clandeftine marriages, and to make the crime of bigamy more difficult to commit; and thofe who choofe to difpenfe with fuch legal forms in their own cafe, thereby fhow, or may be prefumed to fhow, that they have not really confented to be bound by the laws of marriage. But the queftion is, Was the cuftom of holding troth-plight to be equivalent to marriage prevalent in England in Shakefpere's time? There may, of courfe, have been great laxity in this refpect among the lower orders, as there is now; but Shakefpere's family was rather above the lower orders. The Englifh have always been particularly impatient of any attempt to introduce the canon law of marriage, and the famous " Nolumus leges Angliæ mutari " was uttered in oppo-fition to the attempt of the Pope to make the law of England conformable to the principle of the canon law, that a fubfequent marriage renders children born be-fore wedlock legitimate. This was never admitted by Englifh lawyers. But Shakefpere himfelf has recorded his own judgment, and therein the judgment of his day, upon fuch an ante-dating of the public ceremony of matrimony. In " The Tempeft," *Profpero* charges *Ferdinand* and *Miranda*—

> " Then, as my gift, and thine own acquifition
> Worthily purchaf'd, take my daughter : But
> If thou doft break her virgin knot before
> All fanctimonious ceremonies may
> With full and holy rite be minifter'd,
> No fweet afperfion fhall the heavens let fall
> To make this contract grow ; but barren hate,
> Sour-ey'd difdain, and difcord, fhall beftrew
> The union of your bed with weeds fo loathly,
> That you fhall hate it both : therefore, take heed,
> As Hymen's lamps fhall light you."

Whether Shakefpere's married life were a happy one or not, we have no means of knowing; but certainly the circumftances under which it commenced were not promifing.

It has been fuppofed that his bequeathing to his wife only his fecond-beft bed is indicative of no very ftrong affection for her ; but it has been well obferved by Mr. Knight, that this circumftance does not prove much with refpect to the terms on which they lived, becaufe a confiderable part of the property of which he died poffeffed was freehold, and out of this fhe was entitled to her dower and thirds at common law. Still, I cannot help thinking, that had his love for his wife been very ardent or very tender, he would have mentioned her in his will in more endearing terms, and left her fome more fignificant token of affection than his fecond-beft bed.

Anne Hathaway died in 1623, furviving her hufband feven years, and is buried clofe to him in the chancel of the parifh church at Stratford. On her graveftone is this infcription, "Here lyeth interred the body of Anne, wife of William Shakefpeare, who departed this life the 6th day of Auguft, 1623, being of the age of 67 years."

CHAPTER VI.

MARY ARDEN had borne to John Shakespere two
daughters—Joan, born in 1558, the year of Queen
Elizabeth's acceffion; fhe probably died young, as a
fubfequent daughter was chriftened by the fame name.
Margaret, the fecond child, we know, from the regifter,
to have died foon after her birth. William, therefore,
was the eldeft furviving child. He was fucceeded by
Gilbert, born in 1566; Joan, in 1569; Anne, in 1571;
and Edmund, in 1580.

But before the birth of Edmund, John Shakefpere
was beginning to experience the ufual lot of thofe who
have many irons in the fire. In 1578, Afhbies, his
wife's patrimony, was mortgaged. In the next year,
the intereft and reverfion to the eftate at Snitterfield
was fold. When his brother aldermen were required
to contribute fix and eight pence for the equipping of
three pikemen, two billmen, and one archer, John
Shakefpere was indulgently let off for one half, and

was altogether excuſed from contributing fourpence a
week, which the others paid, for the relief of the poor,
then firſt becoming chargeable upon the general public
in conſequence of the diſſolution of the monaſteries.
When, in 1578-9, a rate was levied on the inhabitants
for the purchaſe of armour, he was unable to pay; and
becauſe he had no goods to diſtrain upon, a *capias*
iſſued againſt him on the 19th of January. And then,
of courſe, his embarraſſments came thicker and thicker
upon him, till, at a court held on the 6th September,
1586, a more proſperous citizen was choſen to fill his
place as alderman.

At this time the Poet was twenty-two years of age,
and the gall of this indignity probably entered into his
ſoul, and dictated thoſe bitter taunting reflections of
Jaques, when he ſaw the ſtricken deer deſerted by the
herd:—

> " ' 'Tis right,' quoth he, ' thus miſery doth part
> The flux of company.' Anon a careleſs herd,
> Full of the paſture, jumps along by him,
> And never ſtays to greet him : ' Ay,' quoth Jaques,
> ' Sweep on, you fat and greaſy citizens;
> 'Tis juſt the faſhion; wherefore do you look
> Upon that poor and broken bankrupt there ? ' "

The oſtenſible reaſon of John Shakeſpere's degra-
dation from the poſt of alderman was, that he "dothe
not come to the halles when they be warned, nor

hathe not done of longe time." But, probably, his abfence was caufed by his being in prifon, or in hiding for fear of arreft; for, in the next year, he fued out a writ of *habeas corpus* in the Stratford Court of Record.

From thefe pecuniary embarraffments, and the legal proceedings which fprang out of them, William Shake-fpere probably derived that knowledge of legal terms and practice which, appearing in his plays, led Malone to believe that he was bound apprentice to an attorney; and it is but too likely that he then learnt to count the time by the duration of a law-fuit. " I will devife matter enough," fays *Falftaff*, " out of this *Shallow* to keep *Prince Harry* in continual laughter the wear-ing out of fix fafhions (which is four terms, or two actions), and he fhall laugh without *intervallums.*"

In thefe misfortunes it is to be feared that William Shakefpere was not a comfort or affiftance to his father. Both from the external evidence of tradition, and the internal teftimony of his plays, there is good reafon to fuppofe that his youth was, as the French fay, ftormy. In the archives of Corpus Chrifti College, Oxford, is a collection of antiquarian papers compiled by the Rev. William Fulman, who died in 1688, and who may therefore have been born fome time before Shake-fpere's death. Thefe papers were bequeathed by Mr.

Fulman to his friend, the Rev. Richard Davies, who
died in 1708, and who has added the following remark
on Shakefpere, derived, probably, from information
fupplied to him by his friend. Under the head
" Shakefpere" we read, " Much given to all unlucki-
neffe in ftealing venifon and rabbits, particularly from
Sir —— Lucy, who had him oft whipt, and fometimes imprifoned, and at laft made him fly his native
country, to his great advancement; but his reveng was
fo great, that he is his *Juftice Clodpate* (*i.e.* foolifh
juftice), and calls him a great man; and that, in allufion to his name, bore three lowfes rampant for his
arms." The fame ftory is told by Oldys, Norroy king-
at-arms, and the compiler of the " Biographia Britannica." There was a very aged gentleman living
in the neighbourhood of Stratford (where he died fifty
years fince), who had not only heard from feveral old
people in that town of Shakefpere's tranfgreffion, but
could remember the firft ftanza of that bitter ballad,
which, repeating to one of his acquaintance, he preferved it in writing, and here it is, neither better nor
worfe, but faithfully tranfcribed from the copy which
his relation very courteoufly communicated to me :—

> " A parlemente member, a juftice of peace,
> At home a poor fcare-crowe, at London an affe ;
> If lowfie is Lucy, as fome volk mifcalle it,
> Then Lucy is lowfie, whatever befall it.

He thinks himfelf greate,
Yet an affe in his ftate
We allowe by his ears but with affes to mate.
If Lucy is lowfie, as fome volk mifcalle it,
Sing lowfie Lucy whatever befall it."

Rowe, who wrote the firft life of Shakefpere, and derived his information from Betterton, the actor, gives the following account of the tranfaction :—" An extravagance that he was guilty of forced him both out of the country, and that way of living which he had taken up ; and though it feemed at firft to be a blemifh upon his good manners, and a misfortune to him, yet it afterwards happily proved the occafion of exerting one of the greateft geniufes that ever was known in dramatic poetry. He had, by a misfortune common enough to young fellows, fallen into ill company, and amongft them fome, that made a frequent practice of deer-ftealing, engaged him more than once in robbing a park that belonged to Sir Thomas Lucy, of Charlecote, near Stratford. For this he was profecuted by that gentleman, as he thought, fomewhat too feverely, and, in order to revenge that ill-ufage, he made a ballad upon him. And though this, probably the firft effay of his poetry, be loft, yet it is faid to have been fo very bitter, that it redoubled the profecutions againft him to that degree, that he was obliged to leave his bufinefs and family in Warwick-

ſhire, and ſhelter himſelf in London." A Mr. Thomas
Jones, who lived at Tarbich, a village in Worceſter-
ſhire about eight miles from Stratford, and died in
1703, aged ninety, had often heard the ſame ſtory
from old people at Stratford. So far the external
evidence is as ſtrong as any which is uſually relied
upon under ſuch circumſtances.

The play of "The Merry Wives of Windſor" ſup-
plies internal evidence, not only of a quarrel with Sir
Thomas Lucy, but that the quarrel had its origin in
a poaching affray. The play opens before *Page's*
houſe, at Windſor, where enter *Juſtice Shallow, Slender*, and *Sir Hugh Evans :—*

Shallow. Sir Hugh, perſuade me not; I will make a Star Chamber matter
of it : if he were twenty Sir John Falſtaffs, he ſhall not abuſe Robert
Shallow, eſquire.

Slender. In the county of Glo'ſter, juſtice of peace and *coram.*

Shallow. Ay, couſin Slender, and *Cuſt-alorum.*

Slender. Ay, and *ratolorum* too ; and a gentleman born, maſter parſon ;
who writes himſelf *armigero!* in any bill, warrant, quittance, or obligation, *armigero.*

Shallow. Ay, that I do ; and have done any time theſe three hundred
years.

Slender. All his ſucceſſors gone before him have done 't; and all his an-
ceſtors that come after him may : they may give the *dozen white luces
in their coat.*

Shallow. It is an old coat.

Evans. The dozen white louſes do become an old coat well ; it agrees
well, paſſant ; it is a familiar beaſt to man, and ſignifies love.

Shallow. The luce is a freſh fiſh; the ſalt fiſh is an old coat.

Though the name of the foolifh juftice be *Shallow*, the allufion here to the name and arms of Lucy—arms which the family at Charlecote now bear—is unmiftakable; and, moreover, the very fame ludicrous play upon the words is ufed as in the ftanza of the ballad, which has been preferved. Now for the *corpus delicti* —the matter of the fault.

Falftaff comes in with *Bardolph*, *Nym*, and *Piftol*, and thus addreffes the juftice :—

Falftaff. Now, mafter Shallow, you'll complain of me to the king?
Shallow. Knight, you have beaten my men, killed my deer, and broke open my lodge.
Falftaff. But not kifl'd your keeper's daughter.
Shallow. Tut, a pin! This fhall be anfwer'd.

Malone, and others, feem unwilling to admit this ftory of Shakefpere's youth, and feem to think that it was beneath Shakefpere to be a " deer-ftealer." The word certainly founds bad, but I cannot conceive how anyone could fuppofe that, for a youth to ferret rabbits and kill the fquire's game could imprint a lafting ftigma upon his character. Probably many noblemen who now fit in the Houfe of Lords and pafs gamelaws, have robbed hen-roofts and orchards, and fnared hares, when they were at Harrow or Winchefter, and nobody thinks the worfe of them for it. In the reigns of Elizabeth and James, to break into a park, kill the deer, beat the keeper, and kiſs his pretty daughter, would have been conſidered only in the light of a youthful frolic, and nothing more. Falſtaff, who, in his boyhood, was page to Thomas Mowbray, Duke of Norfolk, and, at the period of " The Merry Wives of Windſor" at leaſt was received at Court, is not the leaſt aſhamed of his exploit.

The truth is, that the guilt of any crime is not meaſured by the crime itſelf, but by the motive and intention of him who commits it. Malice prepenſe is an eſſential element of the crime of murder ; the *animus furandi* of that of larceny. A political aſſaſſination is a great crime ; but the political aſſaſſin may be a high-minded, though miſtaken man ; whereas the ſervant who cuts his maſter's throat that he may rob the till, or the garrotter who ſtrangles a man for his watch, is a baſe ſlave, for whom the moſt ignominious death that can be deviſed is too good. A peaſant who ſteals poultry and kills deer and other game to ſell, that he may live in idleneſs and luxury, is a thief, and deſerves ſome infamous puniſhment ; but a ſchoolboy or youth who, for the ſake of the excitement and adventure, robs a hen-rooſt, or breaks into a deer-park and carries off a buck, is not really a thief. The *animus furandi*, the intention of ſtealing, is not really preſent in his mind. It is rather the love of ſport and the excitement of incurring danger that impels him to do the unlawful act.

We may even go further than this, and affert that the fame act varies in guilt according to the general eftimate of its lawfulnefs or unlawfulnefs at different times; for this reafon, that a man who committed an act univerfally held to be infamous, would be outraging his own confcience, and deftroying his felf-refpect. In Shakefpere's time and long after, the diftinction between the foldier who robbed by wholefale and the poor gentleman who took purfes by retail upon the road, was fcarcely acknowledged; ftill lefs would any note of infamy be attached to a young fellow who fhould turn Robin Hood for the nonce, and infringe the odious foreft-laws.

But, indeed, there is an antecedent probability that young Shakefpere, circumftanced as he was, would be "much given to all unluckinefs;" apt to do wild and daring things which would get him into fcrapes, and live in enmity with the more ftaid and orderly portion of the community. Lord Clive was juft fuch a youth. Lord Byron had the fame aptitude. I do not, of courfe, mean to fay that every man of genius muft neceffarily have been a fcamp when he was young; but it is undoubtedly true, that the fame active imagination and force of will which, when directed to worthy ends, make a man great, will in his hot youth, if he be not reftrained by fome wholefome external influences, hurry him into acts which his mature reafon will condemn. It is when thefe youthful indifcretions are not counterbalanced by nobler counteracting qualities, and therefore form habits which are only ftrengthened by the lapfe of years and become part of the character, that they degrade and corrupt the man. I cannot believe that young Shakefpere can have found an adequate fcope for his energies and afpirations in the farming, butchering, wool-dealing, or gloving, in the profecution of which his father managed to become a bankrupt.

And what more likely form could his wildnefs have affumed than that of unlawful fporting? All Englifhmen are fond of manly out-of-door fports, and no Englifh poet, Chaucer perhaps excepted, has fhown in his works a greater appreciation of the pleafures of the chafe than Shakefpere. It is worth while to cite a few of the many paffages which atteft his practical knowledge and enjoyment of field fports. Here is a defcription of the fhifts of the hare, from one of his earlieft poems, the "Venus and Adonis:"—

> " And when thou haft on foot the purblind hare,
> Mark the poor wretch, to overfhoot his troubles,
> How he outruns the wind, and with what care
> He cranks and croffes with a thoufand doubles:

The many mufits through the which he goes
Are like a labyrinth to amaze his foes.

Sometimes he runs among a flock of fheep,
To make the cunning hounds miftake their fmell ;
And fometimes where earth-delving conies keep,
To ftop the loud purfuers in their yell ;
    And fometimes forteth with a herd of deer :
    Danger devifeth fhifts ; wit waits on fear ;

For there his fmell with others being mingled,
The hot fcent-fnuffing hounds are driven to doubt,
Ceafing their clamorous cry till they have fingled
With much ado the cold fault clearly out ;
    Then do they fpend their mouths : Echo replies,
    As if another chafe were in the fkies.

By this, Poor Wat, far off upon an hill
Stands on his hinder legs with liftening ear,
To hearken if his foes purfue him ftill :
Anon their loud alarums he doth hear :
    And now his grief may be comparèd well
    To one fore fick that hears the paffing-bell.

Then fhalt thou fee the dew-bedabbled wretch
Turn and return, indenting with the way ;
Each envious briar his weary legs doth fcratch,
Each fhadow makes him ftop, each murmur ftay ;
    For mifery is trodden on by many,
    And being low, never relieved by any."

There is a familiarity fhown, too, with the names
of hounds and the terms of hunting in the paffage
where *Profpero* and *Ariel* fet the fpirits on to hunt
Caliban, Stephano, and *Trinculo,* in " The Tempeft."

Profpero. Hey, Mountain, hey!
Ariel. Silver, there it goes, Silver!
Profpero. Fury, Fury! there, Tyrant, there! hark! hark!

Again, in the introduction to "The Taming of a Shrew," the nobleman who comes in from hunting fays—

> Huntfman, I charge thee, tender well my hounds:
> Leach Merriman,—the poor cur is emboffed;
> And couple Clowder with the deep-mouthed brach.
> Saw'ft thou not, boy, how Silver made it good
> At the hedge-corner, in the coldeft fault?
> I would not lofe the dog for twenty pound.
>   *Firft Huntfman.* Why, Belman is as good as he, my lord!
> He cried upon it at the mereft lofs,
> And twice to-day picked out the coldeft fcent:
> Truft me, I take him for the better dog.
>   *Lord.* Thou art a fool: if Echo were as fleet,
> I would efteem him worth a dozen fuch.

Here in two diftinct paffages we have "Silver" ufed as the name of a hound; probably a favourite one of Shakefpere's.

In "A Midfummer Night's Dream" is a charming dialogue on hunting between *Thefeus* and *Hippolyta*:—

>   *Thefeus.* Go, one of you, find out the forefter;
> For now our obfervation is performed;
> And fince we have the vaward of the day,
> My love fhall hear the mufic of my hounds.
> Uncouple in the weftern valley; let them go:
> Defpatch, I fay, and find the forefter.
> We will, fair queen, up to the mountain's top,
> And mark the mufical confufion
> Of hounds and echo in conjunction.

> *Hippolyta.* I was with Hercules and Cadmus once,
> When in a wood of Crete they bayed the bear
> With hounds of Sparta : never did I hear
> Such gallant chiding ; for, befides the groves,
> The fkies, the fountains, every region near,
> Seemed all one mutual cry : I never heard
> So mufical a difcord, fuch fweet thunder.

Thefeus, who poffibly does not like to hear *Hippolyta* fpeak of the pleafant hours fhe fpent with Hercules and Cadmus, and extol their hounds, immediately fays that his hounds, too, are of Sparta, and ftands up for their excellence :—

> " My hounds are bred out of the Spartan kind,
> So flewed, fo fanded ; and their heads are hung
> With ears that fweep away the morning dew.
> Crook-kneed and dew-lapped like Theffalian bulls ;
> Slow in purfuit, but matched in mouth like bells,
> Each under each. A cry more tuneable
> Was never holla'd to, nor cheered with horn,
> In Crete, in Sparta, nor in Theffaly :
> Judge, when you hear."

It is true, thefe crooked-kneed, dew-lapped, long-eared, " tow-rowing " hounds, fo flow in purfuit, would not fuit the ideas of modern fportfmen, who like to come home and talk of, " by Jove, fir, the fafteft thing of fifty minutes you ever faw !" but there is in this paffage an appreciation of the qualities then prized in hounds, which fhows that Shakefpere was a fportfman himfelf, and drew from the life.

For thefe reafons I conclude that Oldys's affertion, that Shakefpere was "much given to all unluckinefs in ftealing venifon and rabbits," is in itfelf probable; and if he did poach upon his neighbours' manors, thofe who know anything of Englifh country gentlemen will not be difpofed to doubt that he was an object of efpecial diflike to the largeft preferver of game in the neighbourhood—that Sir Thomas Lucy who actually brought a bill into Parliament to increafe the ftringency of the game-laws. When it is recollected how young Shakefpere was when he married, and that his unlawful fporting adventures had probably begun when he was ftill at fchool, or foon after, it is not unlikely that Sir Thomas Lucy had had him "whipt;" the imprifonment came afterwards, no doubt.

His mode of revenge was characteriftic, and one which was not unfamiliar to his mind; for he makes *Falftaff* threaten the *Prince* and *Pointz* in "Henry IV." "An I have not ballads made on you all and fung to filthy tunes, let this cup of fack be my poifon." Though the ftanza which has been handed down as the inftrument of his revenge be not of the choiceft, it was enough to anfwer his purpofe. It is founded upon the fame play of words that occurs in "The Merry Wives of Windfor," as already quoted, and is of that rough-and-ready fort that would tickle the ears of an

audience of Warwickfhire clowns, for whom it was
intended. It was alfo likely to be very mortifying to
Sir Thomas Lucy. A county magiftrate like him
would feel infinitely indignant at the bare idea of a
youth like Shakefpere having fo little refpeɛt for him
as to hold up his perfon and name to ridicule; for if
there be one thing more than another which angers
a man to the foul, it is to play upon his name. To
have his "luces," too, of which he was fo proud,
turned into that "beaft" which, however familiar to
man, is "abhorred alike by faint and finner!" It was
more than any county magiftrate could bear. Sir
Thomas Lucy might whip or imprifon young Shakefpere, but young Shakefpere could make Sir Thomas
Lucy a nay-word through the whole country's fide,
fo that wherever his name was mentioned, at fair or
market, men would think of "loufy Lucy;" fuch is
the power of what *Falftaff* calls the "damnable itera-
tion" of the initial letter. But it is curious to fee the
caprice of Fame. A worthy Warwickfhire juftice pro-
fecutes a young farmer for poaching and libelling him
in the groffeft manner. The young farmer incon-
tinently goes to London, and becomes the greateft
poet of one of the greateft nations in the world, and
the worthy country gentleman is handed down to all
pofterity as the perfonification of all that is moft

ridiculous and contemptible in magifterial folly and pretenfion.

There is fome difpute as to the real fcene of Shake-fpere's exploits, but it is probable that he was not particular as to where he fhot his deer or fnared his rabbits.   Mr. Bracebridge maintains, in a pamphlet on the fubject, that Fulbrooke, and not Charlecote, was the fcene of the affray which led to Shakefpere's dif-grace ; but Charlecote was probably only one demefne among many that were laid under contributions.   At any rate, it was the feat of Sir Thomas Lucy, *Mafter Robert Shallow, Efquire,* of the play, and I therefore refolved to pay it a vifit.   !

The road lies over the fine old bridge, built by Sir Hugh Clopton, and along the margin of the Avon, to the left as you leave the town.   As I was walking through a pretty village, I overtook a waggon, and fee-ing that the waggoner looked very much pleafed about fomething, and was evidently anxious to enter into converfation, I determined to indulge him, and " gave him the time of day," as they fay in Effex.   Then it all came out.   There had been a grand harveft-home the day before ; and firft, he told me, the Vicar " prached a farmon for the good of our fowls;" and there was a great tent pitched, and all the people fat at long tables, and there was plenty of beef and plum-pudding ; and " Sir

. Robert H—— was runnin' about till he" (how fhall I tranflate the vigorous but not elegant Anglo-Saxon of my churl?) "perfpired again, afkin' us all, 'Well, have you got anything to ate?' I fuppofe he have been in many a fcrimmage, for he have got a lot o' medals. Then there was all forts of amufement, a band o' mufic and dancin', and throwin' the wheat-fheaf." He added, "Sir Robert is a big man, and a Parliament member." Here we have the very phrafe in the fong. This honeft waggoner and his harveft-home put me in mind of the fheep-fhearing in the "Winter's Tale," when the *Clown* comes in, counting what he has to buy for the feaft :—

"Let me fee, what am I to buy for our fheep-fhearing feaft? Three pound of fugar; five pound of currants; rice—what will this fifter of mine do with rice? But my father hath made her miftrefs of the feaft, and fhe lays it on. She hath made me four-and-twenty nofegays for the fhearers; three-man-fong men all, and very good ones; but they are moft of them means and bafes, but one Puritan amongft them, and he fings pfalms to hornpipes. I muft have faffron, to colour the warden pies; mace, dates—none; that's out of my note; nutmegs, feven; a race or two of ginger; but that I may beg;—four pounds of prunes, and as many of raifins o' the fun."

But ftill more appofite was the churl's defcription of Sir Robert H——'s exertions to pleafe the ruftic guefts to the *Shepherd's* reminifcences of his wife's hofpitable cares :—

" When my old wife lived, upon
This day ſhe was both pantler, butler, cook ;
Both dame and ſervant ; welcomed all ; ſerved all ;
Would ſing her ſong, and dance her turn ; now here
At upper end o' the table, now i' the middle ;
On his ſhoulder, and on his ; her face o' fire
With labour, and the thing ſhe took to quench it."

The ruſtic feaſts, with decorations of flowers and corn, which the gentry are now introducing, are, indeed, only revivals of the old cuſtoms; and Shakeſpere, had he reviſited Stratford in September laſt, would have found himſelf at home among thoſe country merry-makings.

After walking for about three miles, with the Avon on my left, I turned into Charlecote Park, by a clapgate in the maſſive park pales faſtened with trenails with which it is encloſed. It is a noble park, interſperſed with fine oaks and elms, and interſected by the broad, clear Avon, which flows quietly, but not ſluggiſhly along. Preſently I heard the ſmart crack of a rifle, and then a herd of deer made a ruſh paſt me, followed by the boy on an old pony who was driving them to their fate. The keeper was ſhooting a buck. How different was the mode in which the Poet performed the ſame feat! It was a cloth-yard ſhaft that brought his quarry to the ground.

Among the glades of this fine old park, under the

fhade of oaks which were acorns, perhaps, when young Shakefpere was a boy, I felt more fenfibly the prefent divinity than in any other of the fcenes confecrated to his memory. Here Nature's High Prieft was in her temple among the objects of his worfhip, and I was treading the very path which he trod; admiring the very views which he had admired, and looking at the fine old manfion which elicited from him, in the perfon of *Falftaff*, the exclamation, partly of admiration and partly of envy, " 'Fore God, you have a goodly dwelling, and a rich ! "

And, indeed, Charlecote is a noble example of the dwelling of an Englifh country gentleman in the fixteenth and feventeenth centuries. It was built by Sir Thomas Lucy, in 1558, the year of Queen Elizabeth's acceffion. My reader can judge of it from Mr. Edwards's fun-picture, which fhows the front entrance and the pleached garden, where *Mafter Robert Shallow, Efquire*, and his man *Davy* entertained *Falftaff* and his men of war, under the fhrewd conviction that " a friend at court is better than a penny in purfe."

In looking at this fine old manfion—fo light, fo cheerful, fo fuited to the rich Englifh fcenery in which it is planted—I could not help wondering what Lord Macaulay could have meant when he faid that the country gentleman of the feventeenth century " troubled

himself little about decorating his abode, and, if he attempted decoration, seldom produced anything but deformity." This is the historian's estimate of such houses as Charlecote, and Helmingham in Suffolk, and Blickling in Norfolk, and their class, the deformity of which he contrasts with the elegance of those cold, melancholy, barrack-like structures, with a Grecian portico stuck on to them, which, till within the last few years, was considered the right sort of abode for an English gentleman when he went to spend the dull season in the country. But then it must be remembered that the English country gentleman of the sixteenth and seventeenth century was a Tory.

The church is, unfortunately, quite new, having been rebuilt a few years ago by the mother of the present possessor of the estate. It contains, however, the old monuments, amongst which is that erected to commemorate Sir Thomas Lucy, who died in 1595. His recumbent figure in armour, beside his wife, gives one the idea that he was a fine-looking man, and not the starveling described by Shakespere—but marble is deceptive. The "three white Luces" appear everywhere.

A walk across the park and fields by the margin of Avon brought me to my inn at about six o'clock, and so ended one of the pleasantest days of my pilgrimage.

CHAPTER VII.

AND now, in order the better to underftand the procefs by which Shakefpere, having left his beloved Stratford under a cloud, returned to it in a few years, gilded with the funfhine of profperity, we muft accompany him in his expedition to feek his fortunes in London.

In 1583, a few months after his marriage, his eldeft child, Sufanna, was born, and was followed in the fucceeding year by the twins, Judith and Hamnet. A family increafing at this rate, combined with his father's embarraffments, was enough to warn him that he muft beftir himfelf if he would not fink into utter poverty. But perhaps thefe ftrong inducements were quickened by the fear of a profecution by the game-preferving fquire of Charlecote. However this may be, we find him in London in the year 1586 at lateft.

Good fortune, or his inclination, led him, on his arrival, to the theatre. It feems to me extremely probable that he had dabbled in theatrical affairs even before his departure from Stratford. Stage-plays were, before the general diffufion of knowledge, a favourite amufement with the common people, and formed a part of every great feftivity, juft as, before the multiplication of books, ftory-telling was a favourite mode of fpending a winter's evening or a fultry fum-mer's afternoon. He was probably only depicting the immemorial ufage when, in "A Midfummer Night's Dream," he reprefented the "bafe mechanicals" of Athens as welcoming *Thefeus* and *Hippolyta* with a play. In "Love's Labour's Loft," too, a ftage-play is the obvious mode which prefents itfelf to the pedant and the parfon of entertaining the court and fhowing their own wit and learning; and when *Falftaff* wants to be extremly merry, he propofes to the Prince to extemporife a play. I, for one, cannot believe that the Englifh people awoke fuddenly, about the middle of the fixteenth century, to a knowledge and a love of the drama. In one form or other, the people had always had ftage-plays, or ftories in action, at their feftivities; and there can be little doubt that a young fellow like Shakefpere, with the natural proclivity to the drama, which every one muft acknowledge he had, took a part in fuch entertainments of the kind as were performed in his native village. The fame love of amufement which led him into all unluckinefs in

ftealing venifon and rabbits, would alfo lead him to
make one in any projeçt for private theatricals that
might be on foot.

The tafte for the ftage had been for centuries
foftered among all claffes of the Englifh people by the
religious plays, which formed part of the celebration
of the great feafts of the Church. At Chriftmas,
Eafter, and Whitfuntide worldly bufinefs was laid afide
for feveral days, and even weeks. The fovereign and
principal nobility kept their courts with great magni-
ficence at fome favourite palace, and fometimes at a rich
monaftery of which they had been the benefaçtors;
and mafques, plays, and interludes were performed in
their halls by players and muficians, whom they fpecially
retained, and who were therefore called their "fervants." For the general public the Church provided
its Myfteries, Miracles, and Moralities, and thefe were
played in the fpacious naves of cathedrals and minfters,
in inn yards, where the audience might fee them from
the galleries and the chambers, or upon fcaffolds in
market-places.

Antiquaries, of courfe, need not be told what is
meant by Myfteries, Miracles, and Moralities; but as
this little book is intended for the general reader, I
think I had better fay that Myfteries were dramatic
verfions of the great events upon which the Chriftian

religion is founded, fuch as the Nativity, the Paffion, the Refurrection, Afcenfion, and Defcent of the Holy Ghoft at Whitfuntide. Thefe were reduced to the form of a dialogue carried on by the feveral characters, almoft in the very words of Scripture. They are ftill performed in the Tyrol, and laft year feveral letters from tourifts, defcribing them, appeared in the papers. The Miracles were dramatic reprefentations of fome miraculous exertion of Divine power through the intervention of a faint; and the Moralities were allegorical dramas, reprefenting the action of certain virtues and vices perfonified. Several of thefe ancient dramatic works have been collected and publifhed by the Shakefpere Society. Many of them poffefs confiderable humour and dramatic power, and are, indeed, plays to all intents and purpofes, though they are not divided into acts and fcenes. They bear quite as much refemblance to a modern drama as the dialogues recited by the peafants and fhepherds, and faid by Horace to have been invented by Thefpis, did to the Prometheus, the Œdipus, the Medea, and the Nephelæ. Chaucer alludes to the Myfteries when, defcribing *Abfolon*, in the " Milleres Tale," he fays :—

> " Some time, to fhew his lightnefs and maiftrye,
> He playeth Herod on a fcaffold high."

Herod, of courfe, was a character of great prominence

in the Myftery of the Paffion, and fitted to fhow off *Abfolon's* powers. *Hamlet*, too, refers to the fame character in the Myftery when he fays to the players, " O, it offends me to the foul, to hear a robuftious perriwig-pated fellow tear a paffion to tatters, to very rags, to fplit the ears of the groundlings ; who, for the moft part, are capable of nothing but inexplicable dumb fhow, and noife : I would have fuch a fellow whipped for o'erdoing Termagant "—one of the fup-pofed falfe gods of Mahometanifm ; " it out-herods Herod," that is, it overdoes even the overdone character of the perfecuting king of Jews.

When the cuftom of entertaining great people during their vifits to the Univerfities, with an interlude or play, began, I cannot fay, but it probably dates far back beyond the time of Shakefpere. In France, at any rate, not only Myfteries and Miracles were known, but paftoral comedies, fo early as the eleventh century. M. Francifque Michel has publifhed feveral in that moft curious book, his " Théâtre Français du Moyen Age ;" and it can hardly be fuppofed that, at a time when the dukes of Normandy, Touraine, Anjou, and Maine were alfo kings of England, and the nobility and high clergy, of both fides of the Channel, were of the fame race and fpoke the fame language, dramatic amufements fhould be fafhionable in one country and unknown in the other. When people, therefore, speak as if they thought that Englishmen had never heard a tragedy till Sackville and Norton wrote " Gorboduc," or a comedy till Udall wrote " Ralph Roister Doister," or Still " Gammer Gurton's Needle," they seem to me to be talking at random. These may be the first instances of dramatic works reduced to the form of a modern play, but dramas had been known and loved by the people from time immemorial. Indeed, some of the plays of the eleventh century published by M. Francisque Michel are in the original manuscripts set to music, and answer to what we call operas.

The circumstances which produced what may be called the Elizabethan drama are obvious enough. In the middle ages, it need hardly be observed, learning was left almost entirely to the clergy. Every one who followed learning thought it incumbent on him to take orders, because that profession, which included, be it remembered, the practice of the law, alone afforded leisure, opportunity, and remuneration for study. The consequence was, that almost all literature was tinctured with the ecclesiastical spirit, even though it was in many cases directed against the doctrines of the Church and the privileges of the clergy. The drama was not exempt from this general law. It was the monk or the

friar who alone had the leifure or fkill to cater for
the dramatic taftes of the people, and he dramatifed the
Bible, juft as Mr. Terry might dramatife " Rob Roy,"
or Mr. Dion Boucicault " The Collegians." At the
revival, or rather, the diffufion of learning, and efpecially in the countries where the Reformation was
eftablifhed, the clergy ceafed to be an exclufively
learned clafs. The diffolution of the monafteries and
chauntries deprived the Church of the means of providing unambitious graduates of the Univerfities with
a comfortable maintenance immediately on their entrance upon the world, for the parochial cures were
then even lefs appropriately termed " livings " than
now; and the confequence was, that young men
brought the learning they had acquired in the fchools
into general fociety. They did not, as theretofore,
take orders: there was the fame complaint as now,
that young men of promife preferred the chance of
material wealth in worldly profeffions to the ghoftly
riches of the priefthood; and thofe who did affume
the facred office were fo low in the focial fcale that it
was found neceffary to forbid them by a canon to eke
out their living by becoming tapfters. Univerfity
men, like Udall, Still, Greene, Chapman, Peele, and
Marlow, who adopted literature as a profeffion, brought
with them reminifcences of Plautus and Terence, and

perhaps even of Sophocles, Euripides, and Ariftophanes, and no longer derived the perfons of their dramas from fupernatural or faintly beings, Scriptural characters, or abftract virtue and vice, but from profane hiftory and common life. In fhort, the drama did not fpring up all at once in the Englifh nation, but merely, like every other art, received a new development from the great intellectual and focial revolution of the fixteenth century.

With the ftage, therefore, Shakefpere was probably familiar from his youth. We know, indeed, that in 1569, when his father was bailiff, plays were performed in the Town Hall, and it is highly probable that a wild young man of his taftes would feek affociates among "thofe harlotry players," as *Quickly* calls them— the fervants of the earls of Worcefter, Leicefter, or Warwick, for whom the Town Hall was turned into a temporary theatre. And when he found himfelf in London, flenderly provided as we may prefume, he would naturally feek for friends among his old affociates, who were making money lightly at the Globe, Blackfriars, or the Swan, and fpending it as lightly in the "Mermaid," the "Blue Boar," and the "Falcon."

In what capacity he firft obtained employment is uncertain, but it cannot have been a very exalted one. The parifh clerk of Stratford told Dowdall, in 1693,

that he was received into the playhoufe as a ferviture,
which I fuppofe means a fervitor, or, in plain Englifh,
a fervant. This is not inconfiftent with the ftory told
by Sir William Davenant to Betterton, by Betterton to
Rowe, by Rowe to Pope, by Pope to Newton, the
editor of Milton, and by Newton to Johnfon, who
incorporated it in the prolegomena to his edition of
Shakefpere's plays :—" In the time of Elizabeth, coaches
being yet uncommon, and hired coaches not at all in
ufe, thofe who were too proud, too tender, or too idle
to walk, went on horfeback to any diftant bufinefs or
diverfion. Many came on horfeback to the play; and
when Shakefpere fled to London from the terror of a
criminal profecution, his firft expedient was to wait at
the door of the playhoufe and hold the horfes of thofe
that had no fervants, that they might be ready again
after the performance. In this office he became fo
confpicuous for his care and readinefs, that in a fhort
time every man as he alighted called for ' Will Shakefpere,' and fcarcely any other waiter was trufted with a
horfe to hold while Will Shakefpere could be had.
This was the firft dawn of better fortune. Shakefpere
finding more horfes put into his hand than he could
hold, hired boys to wait under his infpection, who,
when Will Shakefpere was fummoned, were immediately to prefent themfelves—'*I am Will Shakefpere's*

boy, fir.' In time Shakefpere found higher employment; but as long as the practice of riding to the
playhoufe continued, the waiters that held the horfes
retained the appellation of *Shakefpere's boys.*"

Whether this ftory be true or not, it certainly is not
improbable. To take the firft employment that offered
any remuneration, and to diftinguifh himfelf even in
the humble office of holding horfes, is eminently characteriftic of the practical good fenfe of the man who,
while compofing works requiring the exercife of the
higheft and moft cultivated imagination and tafte, was
bringing actions for his rents, buying up impropriate
tithes, and making money of his wheat, fheep, and
beeves. Money was his prefling need at the time, not
only for himfelf, but for the wife and young family
whom he had left at Stratford; money was to be got
honeftly by holding gentlemen's horfes—and he held
them.

A man "whofe blood and judgment were" not "fo
well commingled," would have been deprefied by the
meannefs of his employment; but Shakefpere knew
that in order to climb to the top of the ladder you
muft begin at the bottom, and went on mounting
fteadily and furely till he had arrived at the height to
which he intended to attain. With that tafte which,
in one of his education is even more wonderful than his

creative genius, he perceived the deficiencies of the plays which then held the ftage. His predeceffors were Udall, Heywood, Still, Redford, Ingelend, Munday, the two Wagers, Lyly, the euphuift; but Peele, Greene, Lodge, Nafh, Marlowe, Kyd, Daniel, Belchier, Clarke, and Wilfon were alfo his contemporaries, and though many of their plays fhow confiderable merit, befide the great Mafter—him who held the horfes of the gallants who came to hear their plays—they muft pale their ineffectual fires. Greene's "Looking Glafs for London and England" is more admirable in its comic than its tragic parts; but it is a fine play, full of fierce invective, which was his forte. "Friar Bacon and Friar Bungay" has fome pretty and fome effective fcenes; but one feels painfully throughout that, after one has been led up with great care and preparation to a point, the point is feebly made, or not at all. Peele's "David and Bethfabe" is perhaps better than "Titus Andronicus;" but "Edward I." is not to be compared with the worft of Shakefpere's hiftorical plays. The "Old Wives' Tale" is really a pretty piece of faerie, and there is fomething myfterious and grand in the unintelligible incantations at the well; but how infinitely is it left behind by *Oberon*, *Puck*, and *Titania*, by the weird fifters in "Macbeth," and by *Ariel* and *Caliban !* "The Devil and Dr. Fauftus," by Marlowe, is much admired, but it always seems to me as if the *Doctor* was too palpably cheated. He really gets nothing in exchange for his soul. Goethe's *Faust* does enjoy himself for the time, but Marlowe's *Dr. Faustus* wearies the reader by his continual anticipation of the day of reckoning. The whole interest and tragic effect of the play is produced by his repentance of the bargain he has made from the very moment when it has been ratified.

Shakespere's first employment in the higher business of the theatre is supposed to have been the correcting and adapting for the stage the imperfect plays of his contemporaries. In 1592 Robert Greene ended his wretched life in misery, and, as his last act, bequeathed his " Groat's worth of Wit bought with a Million of Repentance "—a malignant libel under the hypocritical mask of a charitable warning—to his fellows in talent and profligacy, Marlowe, Lodge, and Peele. This strange effusion—of which I scarcely know whether to admire the power of the language, or wonder at the ghastly spectacle it presents of a profligate pouring curses with his failing breath upon the companions of his vices —contains the following address to Peele, in which there is an obvious allusion to Shakespere, as the publisher afterwards acknowledged :—" And thou, no less deserving than the other two (Marlowe and Lodge), in some things rarer, in nothing inferior, driven, as myfelf, to extraordinary fhifts, a little have I to fay to thee; and were it not an idolatrous oath, I would fwear by fweet St. George thou art unworthy better hap, fith thou dependeſt on fo mean a ſtay. Bare-minded men all three of you, if by my mifery ye be not warned; for unto none of you like me fought thofe burs to cleave; thofe puppets I mean that fpeak from our mouths, thofe anticks garnifhed in our colours. Is it not ſtrange that I, to whom they all have been beholding; is it not like that you, to whom they all have been beholding, fhall, were you in that cafe that I am now, be both of you at once forfaken? Yes, truſt them not, for there is an upſtart now beautified with our feathers, that, with his tiger's heart wrapt in a player's hide, fuppofes he is as well able to bombaſt out a blank verfe as the beſt of you; and being an abfolute *Johannes Factotum*, is, in his own conceit, the only *Shake-fcene* in a country."

The expreſſion, "Tiger's heart wrapt in a player's hide," is a parody of a line in the third part of "King Henry the Sixth," Act I., Sc. 4—

"Oh, tiger's heart wrapp'd in a woman's hide!"

And there is no poſſibility of doubting that *Shake-fcene* is an allufion to the name of Shakefpere. From this it may be concluded that in fix years after coming to London, Shakefpere had eftablifhed fuch a reputation as an actor that he had become the object of Greene's impotent jealoufy ; that he had made himfelf fo ufeful to the theatre as to be confidered a *Johannes Factotum :* an author as well as an actor, able to fhake the houfe, and to rival "Marlowe's mighty line." But whether the expreffion, "a crow beautified with our feathers," means only that he obtained profit and applaufe by acting the plays which they had written, or that he retouched them, or borrowed from them, is doubtful. Certain it is that he was an object of diflike to the profligate fet of whom Greene was one—partly, no doubt, becaufe he exhibited a felf-refpect and fore-thought which were a tacit reproach to their debauchery and improvidence.

This malignant outburft of envy on the part of Greene was the means of eliciting the teftimony of Chettle, the publifher, to the high character that Shakefpere bore amongft his contemporaries; and this, is the more valuable as Marlowe is excepted from the like praife. Chettle appears to have really meant what he faid of Shakefpere. The two aggrieved authors, as it feems, remonftrated with Chettle for publifhing this attack upon them, and this is his reply:—"With neither of them that take offence (Shakefpere and

Marlowe) was I acquainted, and with one of them I
care not if I never be : the other, whom at that time I
did not fo much fpare as fince I wifh I had—for that,
as I have moderated the heat of living writers, and
might have ufed my own difcretion, efpecially in fuch
a cafe, the author being dead—that I did not I am as
forry as if the original fault had been my fault, becaufe
myfelf have feen his demeanour no lefs civil than
he excellent in the quality he profeffes. Befides
divers of worfhip have reported his uprightnefs of
dealing, which argues his honefty, and his facetious
grace in writing, which approves his art." As to
Shakefpere's excellence in his art we need not Chettle's
teftimony, but it is pleafant to find that the moral
qualities for which he was refpected by his contemporaries were uprightnefs and courtefy; nor is it fmall
praife to fay that he knew how to pleafe men of ftation
and good breeding.

It luckily happens that in a pedantic and euphuiftic
treatife on the poets of England, called "Palladis
Tamia, Wit's Treafury, being the Second Part of Wit's
Commonwealth," written by Francis Meeres, and publifhed in 1598, we find an authentic record of the
plays and poems which had been produced by Shakefpere up to that period. Here is the paffage :—" As the
foule of Euphorbus was thought to live in Pythagoras,

ſo the ſweete wittie ſoule of Ovid lives in melli-
fluous and hony-tongued Shakeſpeare; witneſs his
' Venus and Adonis,' his ' Lucrece,' his ſugred Sonnets
among his private friends. . . . . As Plautus and Seneca
are accounted the beſt for comedy and tragedy among
the Latines, ſo Shakeſpeare among the Engliſh is the
moſt excellent in both kinds for the ſtage; for comedy,
his ' Gentlemen of Verona,' his ' Errors' [" Comedy of
Errors"], his ' Love Labors Loſt,' his ' Love Labors
Won' [" All's Well that Ends Well"], his ' Midſummer
Night Dreame,' and his ' Merchant of Venice;' for
tragedy, his ' Richard the Second,' ' Richard the Third,'
' Henry the Fourth,' ' King John,' ' Titus Andronicus,'
and his ' Romeo and Juliet.'" To theſe original, or
nearly original, plays, may be added his re-caſts of
" Pericles," " Henry the Sixth," firſt part; " Henry the
Sixth," ſecond part; " Henry the Sixth," third part.
The three parts of " Henry the Sixth" were all originally
written by the unfortunate Kit Marlowe, whoſe pretty
ſong, " Come live with me and be my love," is ſung by
Sir Hugh Evans in " The Merry Wives of Windſor,"
to keep up his courage when he is going to fight with
Dr. Caius, and by the Milkmaid in Iſaac Walton's
" Complete Angler." They were merely touched up
and adapted for the ſtage by the " Johannes Factotum "
at the theatre at Blackfriars.

From this, then, we learn that Shakefpere, at the age of thirty-four, had written "Venus and Adonis," "The Rape of Lucrece," his Sonnets, amounting to one hundred and fifty-four, befides twelve original plays, and that he had altered and adapted four or five more. All this time he was alfo gaining money by acting.

In thofe times the profits of literary labour were not fo great as now. We all remember the price for which Milton fold the copyright of the "Paradife Loft" in the next century. But the reign of Queen Elizabeth was the tranfition period between a liftening and a reading age; the theatre was ftill the great vehicle through which the poet reached the public ear, and play-writing was probably the beft paid of any literary labour. Of this a curious example is to be found in a novel called "Never too Late," written by Greene, the dramatift, and believed by Mr. Dyce to be the hiftory of his wretched life. The hero, *Roberto*, is reduced to great fhifts, and is bewailing his wretched fate behind a hedge :—

"On the other fide of the hedge fat one that heard his forrow, who, getting over, came towards him and brake off his paffion. When he approached, he faluted Roberto in this fort, ' Gentleman,' quoth he, ' for fo you feem, I have by chance heard you difcourfe fome part of your grief, which appeareth to me more than

you will difcover or I can conceit. But if you vouch-
fafe fuch fimple comfort as my ability will yield, affure
yourfelf that I will endeavour to do the beft that either
may procure your profit or bring you pleafure; the
rather for that I fuppofe you are a fcholar, and pity
it is men of learning fhould live in lack.' Roberto,
wondering to hear fuch good words, for that this
iron age affords few that efteem of virtue, returned
him thankful gratulations, and, urged by neceffity,
uttered his prefent grief, befeeching his advice how
he might be employed. ' Why, eafily,' quoth he, ' and
greatly to your benefit; for men of my profeffion get
by fcholars their whole living.' ' What is your profeffion?' faid Roberto. ' Truly, fir,' faid he, ' I am a
player.' ' A player!' quoth Roberto; ' I took you rather
for a gentleman of great living; for if by outward
habit men fhould be cenfured [judged], I tell you, you
would be taken for a fubftantial man.' ' So am I,
where I dwell,' quoth the player, ' reputed able at
my proper coft to build a windmill. What though
the world once went hard with me, when I was fain
to carry my playing fardel afoot-back? [to carry my
properties on my back as I walked.] *Tempora mutantur:*
—I know you know the meaning of it better than I—but
I thus confter it, *It is otherwife now;* for my very fhare
in playing apparel will not be fold for two hundred

pounds.' 'Truly,' faid Roberto, 'it is ftrange that you
fhould fo profper in that vain practice, for that it feems
to me your voice is nothing gracious.' 'Nay then,'
faid the player, 'I miflike your judgment; why, I am
as famous for *Delphrygus* and the *King of Fairies* as
ever was any of my time; "The Twelve Labours of
Hercules" have I terribly thundered on the ftage, and
played three fcenes of "The Devil on the Highway
to Heaven."' 'Have you fo?' faid Roberto, 'then I
pray you pardon me.' 'Nay, more,' quoth the player,
'I can ferve to make a pretty fpeech, for I was a.
country author, paffing at a Moral [a Morality]; for
it was I that penned "The Moral of Man's Wit,"
"The Dialogue of Doves," and for feven years' fpace
was abfolute interpreter of the puppets. But now my
almanack is out of date—

> "The people make no eftimation
> Of Morals, teaching education."

Was not this pretty for a plain rhyme extempore? If
ye will, you fhall have more.' 'Nay, it is enough,'
faid Roberto; 'but how mean you to ufe me?' 'Why,
fir, in making plays,' faid the other; 'for which you
fhall be well paid, if you will take the pains.' Roberto,
perceiving no remedy, thought it beft to refpect [have
regard to] his prefent neceffity, and, to try his wit, went
with him willingly; who lodged him at the town's

end, &c. &c. . . . But Roberto, now famoufed for an arch play-making poet, his purfe, like the fea, fometimes fwelled—anon, like the fame fea, fell to a low ebb; yet feldom he wanted, his labours were fo well efteemed."

If Greene, with vaftly inferior powers and induftry, were able, by writing plays only, to fet want at defiance, notwithftanding his extravagant and thriftlefs mode of life, it is no wonder that Shakefpere, with his extraordinary induftry, his prudence, and the combined profits of writing for the ftage and acting, fhould have foon raifed himfelf to a good pofition, fo that he was reputed where he dwelt, and indeed was, "able at his proper coft to build a windmill," or to buy the beft houfe in his native town.

CHAPTER VIII.

WE have followed Shakefpere from Stratford to the playhoufe, where he is enjoying not only the light froth of popular applaufe, but the folid pudding of fubftantial profit. We have feen him begin by holding the horfes of gentlemen who rode to the play, and rifing gradually from amending and adapting the works of others to be himfelf a great dramatic writer and actor, and, in fact, the founder of the modern drama. We naturally inquire what fort of playhoufes were thofe in which his mafterpieces firft appeared ? With what fcenery and other means and appliances were thofe dramas, which now require all the art of the machinift, the fcene painter, and the upholfterer, to make them tolerable to our faftidious age, firft prefented to the wits and courtiers of the days of Elizabeth and James ?

The playhoufes in which the pageantry of " Henry the Eighth " and " Macbeth," and the fairy fcenes of " The Tempeft " and " A Midfummer Night's

Dream," were firſt reprefented, were little better than
wooden ſheds. I do not believe that they were deftitute of a certain architectural beauty of their own,
for in that time the old art-traditions of the middle
ages had not yet been utterly loſt; and they were
probably much better adapted to their purpofe than
our great, fuffocating, uncomfortable theatres, where,
what with the fize of the houfe and the mumbling and
ranting of the actors, it is impoffible to hear one word
in ten ; but they were totally deſtitute of ſcenery.
Curtains, or, as they were called, "traverfes," fupplied
the place of ſcenes ; the ſtage was ſtrewed with ruſhes ;
at the back of the ſtage was a balcony, raiſed eight
or nine feet from the ground, which ferved as an upper
chamber or window, from whence, as in "Romeo and
Juliet," a part of the dialogue might be ſpoken ; and
the ceiling, called the "heavens," was painted blue, as
in the churches of the time. The ſtage was hung with
black when a tragedy was performed. A bed placed
upon it indicated that the ſcene was a bed-chamber ; a
table with pen and ink denoted a counting-houfe. Trap-
doors and pulleys were fometimes ufed, but were not
effential. The place of action was written on a board
for the information of the audience. Inſtead of the
prompter's bell, a flouriſh of trumpets announced that
the curtain which feparated the ſtage from the audience

was about to be drawn, and at the third founding the play began.

The audience were not perhaps fo well accommodated as at prefent. In the public theatres the area, called the "yard," was open to the fky, and no part of the houfe was roofed but the ftage and boxes; in the private houfes the whole was covered in. The ftage was feparated from the pit or yard by pales, within which young men of fafhion ufed to fit on ftools, and criticife the performance. The orcheftra was fituated in the place now occupied by the ftage-boxes. The remainder of the audience was accommodated, as with us, in private boxes and galleries, or fcaffolds.

In Shakefpere's time there were no lefs than eleven theatres in London. There was The Theatre, fo called by way of diftinction, Paris Garden, the Globe, the Rofe, the Hope, the Swan, in Southwark, the Black-friars, the Whitefriars, the Fortune, in Golden Lane, and the Red Bull.

The dreffes of the players were fometimes very rich. We have feen that the player's wardrobe, in Greene's "Never too Late," was worth two hundred pounds. Women never acted till after the Reftoration, and female parts were played by boys, generally the chorifters from the church or royal chapel, as they are now at the Weftminfter plays. This muft have been the moft ferious defect in the Elizabethan acted drama. And yet, when one obferves the continual effort of all but the beft actreffes to attract perfonal admiration, one cannot but acknowledge that both plans have their difadvantages.

Hamlet's directions to the players, the play within the play, and fome of Jonfon's comedies, afford the beft idea of the cuftoms of the players and audience. From *Hamlet's* directions to the players we learn that the clowns fometimes, as indeed they do now, extemporifed a joke to bring down a laugh—

"And let thofe that play your clown fpeak no more than is fet down for them; for there be of them that will themfelves laugh, to fet on fome quantity of barren fpectators to laughter; though, in the meantime, fome neceffary queftion of the play be then to be confidered "—

and that the principal actors wore periwigs—

" O, it offends me to the foul to hear a robuftious periwig-pated fellow tear a paffion to tatters."

From the play, we fhould conclude that young men of fafhion criticifed the performance aloud in a very rude and unceremonious manner, as where *Hamlet* fays to the actor on the ftage—

" Begin, murderer—leave thy damnable faces, and begin ! "

From Jonfon's comedies we learn that the audience took tobacco, that is, fmoked without remorfe; that, indeed, did not fignify fo much when the pit was *fub Jove frigido.*

The prices of admiffion to the boxes were a fhilling, and to the yard or pit and galleries, fixpence, fourpence, twopence, and even a penny. The play began after dinner, or at "undern of the day," or "under meles," that is, about three o'clock; and people, therefore, got home, or to the tavern, as the cafe might be, at about feven to fupper.

Thefe arrangements would be confidered rather rude and uncomfortable by modern play-goers; but then it muft be remembered that plays were continually acted at Court, to which everybody of note at that time re-forted, and in the houfes of the high nobility; and, in the independence in which the drama ftood of fcenical decorations, the great dining-hall or prefence chamber could be converted into a theatre in a very fhort time, by merely hanging a few pieces of tapeftry acrofs the apartment.

And now the further queftion arifes, was juftice done to Shakefpere's plays in fuch theatres, and with fuch lack of fcenery? I fhould anfwer, without hefitation, yes. For myfelf, I am of Charles Lamb's opinion, that Shakefpere's plays are more enjoyed in the reading than in the beholding. I have often feen "Hamlet" and "King Richard the Third," and to my mind *Hamlet*

and *Richard* have become identified with Mr. Charles
Kean. Thank goodnefs! I have never feen "Lear." I
fhould be forry indeed to have my ideal of the hale,
impulfive, fomewhat boifterous and paffionate old king,
firft driven mad, then foftened and refined by his great
forrow and tender love, deftroyed by fome periwig-pated
fellow. But if aƈted at all, let the words of the Poet,
and not the drefs and fcenery, be relied upon to produce
their effeƈt. As between tawdry, vulgar, inappropriate
fcenery and dreffes, and the correƈt and tafteful decorations of the Princefs's during Mr. Kean's management,
there can be no comparifon. But, in my opinion, fimple
traverfes, or curtains, and the quiet, rich, unpedantic
dreffes of the Elizabethan drama, would be better than
either. If managers would fpend lefs money upon
fcenery, and more upon fecuring the higheft dramatic
attainment in the performers; and if aƈtors would think
more of ftudying their parts and declaiming them
correƈtly, and lefs of their flafhed doublets and flefh-
coloured tights, Shakefpere would be more worthily
reprefented on the ftage.

Homer makes his model orator mean in his appearance, awkward in his geftures, and totally deftitute of
aƈtion, fo that people thought he was a fool until he
opened his mouth; and then every eye was turned
upon him, and every mind was bowed by the perfuafion

of his voice. I have always thought this a high ftroke of criticifm—an ideal which would never have occurred to any but a mafter. If the orator cannot make an impreffion by his words and the intonation of his voice, he will never do it by " fawing the air." Juft fo, what one defiderates on the ftage is to have Shake-fpere's fpeeches fpoken as they are fet down, with all the advantages of emphafis and intonation which the natural aptitude, the ftudy, and the practice of the actor can give them; but who cares, or ought to care, what drefs the player wears, or whether the painted caftle on the fcene have the appropriate dog-toothed moulding of the reign of King John or not? I think, therefore, that Queen Elizabeth and King James and their courtiers, and the audiences which crowded the playhoufe at Black-friars and the Globe, probably faw Shakefpere's plays to as great advantage as we are ever likely to do, and perhaps to greater. At any rate, they did not fee Shake-fpere infulted by Cibber's and Garrick's interpolations. They were never treated to—" Off with his head! So much for Buck-ing-ham!"

Shakefpere had got him " a fellowfhip in a cry of players," known as " the Lord Chamberlain's fervants." They poffeffed two theatres, one at Blackfriars, oppo-fite the place where Apothecaries' Hall now ftands; here they played in winter, becaufe it was effectually protected from the weather. At the Globe, on the Bankſide, they played in ſummer. A petition, ſtill extant, dated 1596, and addreſſed by the proprietors to the Privy Council, praying to be allowed to repair the houſe and continue their entertainments at the theatre in Blackfriars, proves that Shakeſpere was a ſhareholder in the concern, in conjunction with Thomas Pope, Richard Burbage, John Hemings, Auguſtine Phillips, Wm. Kempe, Wm. Slye, and Nicholas Tooley. As to his attainments as an actor, the traditions are various and conflicting. Chettle ſays, as we have ſeen, that he was "excellent in the quality he profeſſeth;" Aubrey, that he "did act exceedingly well;" Wright, that "he was a much better poet than player." There can be little doubt of that, unleſs he was the greateſt player that ever trod the ſtage. He adds, however, and this is obviouſly an error, "I could never meet with any further account of him this way than that the top of his performance was the *Ghoſt*, in his own 'Hamlet.'" Oldys ſays that a younger brother of the Poet's, who lived at Stratford to a good old age, uſed to tell how he ſaw Shakeſpere play the part of "an old man, who was carried by another perſon to a table, at which he was ſeated among ſome company who were eating, and that one of them ſang a ſong." This obviouſly points to *Adam*, in "As You Like It."

There is a tradition that King James, flattered by the lines fo complimentary to himfelf in " Henry the Eighth "—

"Nor fhall this peace fleep with her; but as when
The bird of wonder dies, the maiden phœnix,
Her afhes new create another heir,
As great in admiration as herfelf,
So fhall fhe leave her bleffednefs to one
(When heaven fhall call her from this cloud of darknefs)
Who, from the facred afhes of her honour
Shall, ftar-like, rife as great in fame as fhe was,
And fo ftand fixed: peace, plenty, love, truth, terror,
That were the fervants to this chofen infant,
Shall then be his, and like a vine grow to him.
Wherever the bright fun of heaven fhall fhine,
His honour and the greatnefs of his name
Shall be, and make new nations: he fhall flourifh,
And, like a mountain cedar, reach his branches
To all the plains about him. Our children's children
Shall fee this, and blefs heaven"—

"was pleafed with his own hand to write an amicable letter to Mr. Shakefpere;" which letter, though now loft, remained long in the hands of Sir William Davenant, "as a creditable perfon, now living, can teftify." This is Lintot's ftatement, and Oldys, in a note on Fuller's Worthies, fays that Lintot's authority for this was Sheffield, Duke of Buckingham, who faw the letter in Davenant's poffeffion. This is certain, from the " Accounts of the Revels at St. James's," in the reign of James, that Shakefpere's plays were frequently performed at Court.

Amongſt the nobility of that time the theatre was a very popular amuſement. Of this we have a curious proof in the Sydney Papers. Rowland Whyte, in a letter to Sir Robert Sydney, ſays :—" My Lord Southampton and Lord Rutland came not to the Court; the one doth but very ſeldom ; they paſs away the time in London merely in going to plays every day."

Southampton's reaſon for not going to Court was that his friend Eſſex was then in priſon and diſgrace ; but the way in which he ſolaced himſelf indicates his taſte. This is the Southampton to whom Shakeſpere dedicated his earlieſt poems, " Venus and Adonis " and " The Rape of Lucrece ;" and the dedications are ſo characteriſtic, that I think they will help much in forming an eſtimate of Shakeſpere. The Dedication of the " Venus and Adonis " is addreſſed to the Right Honourable Henry Wriotheſly, Earl of Southampton and Baron of Tichfield, and is as follows :—

" Right Honourable,—I know not how I ſhall offend in dedicating my unpoliſhed lines to your lordſhip, nor how the world will cenſure me for chooſing ſo ſtrong a prop to ſupport ſo weak a burden ; only, if your honour ſeem but pleaſed, I account myſelf highly praiſed, and vow to take advantage of all idle hours till I have honoured you with ſome graver labours. But if the firſt heir of my invention prove deformed, I ſhall be ſorry it had ſo noble a godfather, and never after ear [plough] ſo barren a land, for fear it yield me ſtill ſo bad a harveſt. I leave it to your honourable ſurvey, and your honour to your heart's content, which I wiſh may always anſwer your own wiſh and the world's hopeful expectation.—Your honour's in all duty,　　" WILLIAM SHAKESPERE."

The dedication of "The Rape of Lucrece" is addreffed to the fame accomplifhed nobleman :—

"The love I dedicate to your lordfhip is without end; whereof this
pamphlet, without beginning, is but a fuperfluous moiety. The warrant
I have of your honourable difpofition, not the worth of my untutored
lines, makes it affured of acceptance. What I have done is yours; what
I have to do is yours; being part in all I have, devoted yours. Were
my worth greater, my duty would fhow greater; meantime, as it is, it is
bound to your lordfhip, to whom I wifh long life, ftill lengthened with
all happinefs."

There appears to me to be in thefe complimentary
addreffes a more manly and independent fpirit, lefs
deformed by extravagant conceits, than is to be found
in moft dedications of the period. In the firft, Shakefpere does not hefitate to fay, that he hopes to honour
his patron by fome graver work. This hope was not
fulfilled, perhaps, as he intended it; but the memory
of Southampton is certainly moft honoured in the
record of his friendfhip for the Poet.

The fecond feems to indicate a growing intimacy
and affection. This affection is faid to have been fo
great on Southampton's fide, that he once prefented
Shakefpere with a thoufand pounds to carry through a
purchafe in which he was then engaged, poffibly a
fhare in the Blackfriars or the Globe. Now a thoufand pounds in the time of Queen Elizabeth was worth
fully as much as five thoufand now. This would have
been a very large gift to one in Shakefpere's circum-

ftances; but that the tradition exifted in the time of Sir William Davenant is fufficient ground for believing that Southampton did make Shakefpere a handfome prefent, though we may allow fomething for exaggeration as to the amount.

The fubjects of both thefe poems are fuch, that an edition of Shakefpere which contains them cannot be left upon a drawing-room table. I think my readers will therefore be obliged to me if I extract a few of the moft ftriking paffages from both. They are Shakefpere's earlieft productions: the "Venus and Adonis" he calls the "firft heir of my invention."

The defcription of Adonis's hounds returning after having loft their mafter and brought the boar to bay is extremely graphic, and further illuftrates the Poet's intimate knowledge of hunting:—

> " By this fhe hears the hounds are at a bay,
>   Whereat fhe ftarts, like one that fpies an adder,
>   Wreathed up in fatal folds juft in his way,
>   The fear whereof doth make him fhake and fhudder;
>   Even fo the timorous yelping of the hounds
>   Appals her fenfes, and her fpirit confounds.

> " For now fhe knows it is no gentle chafe,
>   But the blunt boar, rough bear, or lion proud,
>   Becaufe the cry remaineth in one place,
>   Where fearfully the dogs exclaim aloud:
>   Finding their enemy to be fo curft,
>   They all ftrain courtefy who fhall cope him firft.
>   *   *   *   *   *

" Here kennelled in a brake fhe finds a hound,
　And afks the weary caitiff for his mafter;
　And then another licking of his wound,
　　'Gainft venomed fores the only fovereign plafter ;
　　And here fhe meets another fadly fcowling,
　　To whom fhe fpeaks, and he replies with howling.

" When he hath ceafed his ill-refounding noife,
Another flap-mouthed mourner, black and grim,
Againft the welkin vollies out his voice ;
Another and another anfwer him,
　Clapping their proud tails to the ground below,
　Shaking their fcratched ears, bleeding as they go."

No one who had not clofely obferved hounds could
have written this.　The conclufion almoft rifes to fub-
limity in the picture it draws of the dire evils which
attend upon earthly paffion :—

" Since thou art dead, lo, here I prophefy,
　Sorrow on love hereafter fhall attend :
　It fhall be waited on with jealoufy,
　Find fweet beginning, but unfavoury end ;
　　Ne'er fettled equally, but high or low,
　　That all love's pleafure fhall not match his woe.

" It fhall be fickle, falfe, and full of fraud ;
　Bud and be blafted in a breathing while;
　The bottom poifon, and the top o'erftrewed
　With fweets that fhall the trueft fight beguile ;
　　The ftrongeft body fhall it make moft weak,
　　Strike the wife dumb, and teach the fool to fpeak.

" It fhall be fparing and too full of riot,
　Teaching decrepit age to tread the meafures ;

The ftaring ruffian fhall it keep in quiet,
Pluck down the rich, enrich the poor with treafures;
    It fhall be raging mad and filly mild,
    Make the young old, the old become a child.

" It fhall fufpeƈt where is no caufe of fear;
It fhall not fear where it fhould moft miftruft ;
It fhall be merciful, and too fevere,
And moft deceiving when it feems moft juft ;
    Perverfe it fhall be where it fhows moft toward,
    Put fear to valour, courage to the coward."

This is quite in the manner of the old Englifh poets, and reminds one of the moral to the beautifully told but licentious ftory of " January and May," in Chaucer's " Canterbury Tales." Pluto threatens to make known the guilt of May, when Proferpine thus addreffes him, and, in her fpeech, points the moral of the tale :—

" ' Ye fhall,' quoth Proferpine, ' and will ye fo ?
Now, by my mother Ceres' foul I fwear
That I fhall give her fuffifant anfwèr,
And allè women after, for her fake ;
That though they be in any guilt itake,
With facè bold they fhall themfelves excufe,
And bear them down that woulden them accufe ;
For lack of anfwer none of them fhall dien.
All had you feen a thing with both your eyen,
Yet fhall we women vifage it hardily,
And weep, and fwear, and chidè fubtilly,
That ye fhall be as lewed [foolifh] as be geefe.' "

Both the fentiments, the idea of indicating the moral of the tale, and the vigour of the language, are alike in both. But there is a ftill more ftriking refem-

blance, perhaps, in one of the expreffions in the paffage
quoted, to a bitter ftanza in another of Chaucer's poems,
" The Court of Love :"—

> " For it peràdventure may fo befall
> That they [women] be bound by nature to deceive,
> And fpin and weep, and *fugar ftrew on gall,*
> The heart of man to ravifh and to reave."

Compare with this :—

> " The bottom poifon, and the top o'erftrewed
> With fweets that fhall the trueft fight beguile."

" The Rape of Lucrece " is a far nobler and more
varied poem. There can be little doubt that Shakefpere was indebted to the *Legenda Lucrecie Rome,
Martyris,* in Chaucer's " Legende of Gode Women,"
for its general idea, and for many of the thoughts. It
abounds with fine paffages ; but I will choofe the
defcription of the picture in the houfe of Collatinus,
becaufe it fhows that even thus early in his career the
Poet loved and appreciated the kindred art of painting :

> " At laft fhe calls to mind where hangs a piece
> Of fkilful painting made for Priam's Troy.
> *   *   *   *
> A thoufand lamentable objects there,
> In fcorn of Nature, art gave lifelefs life ;
> Many a dry drop feemed a weeping tear,
> Shed for the flaughtered hufband by the wife ;
> The red blood reeked to fhow the painter's ftrife ;
>   And dying eyes gleamed forth their afhy lights,
>   Like dying coals burnt out in tedious nights.

"There might you fee the labouring pioneer
Begrimed with fweat and fmearèd all with duft ;
And from the towers of Troy there would appear
The very eyes of men through loopholes thruft,
Gazing upon the Greeks with little luft :
   Such fweet obfervance in this work was had,
   That one might fee thofe far-off eyes look fad.

"In great commanders grace and majefty
You might behold triumphing in their faces ;
In youth quick bearing and dexterity ;
And here and there the painter interlaces
Pale cowards, marching on with trembling paces ;
   Which heartlefs peafants did fo well refemble,
   That one would fwear he faw them quake and tremble.

"In Ajax and Ulyffes, oh ! what art
Of phyfiognomy might one behold !
The face of either ciphered either's heart ;
Their face their manners moft exprefly told :
In Ajax' eyes blunt rage and rigour rolled ;
   But the mild glance that fly Ulyffes lent
   Showed deep regard and fmiling government."

How admirable is the contraft between the mere
foldier and the ftatefman ! How expreffive the phrafe,
"blunt rage!" and how exactly does it defcribe the
character of Ajax, as drawn by Homer ! The "mild
glance" of "fly Ulyffes" reminds one of the "Mitis
fapientia Læli ;" but the "deep regard and fmiling
government" are Shakefpere's own, and fhow that he
had feen and marked the deportment of thofe great
ftatefmen who fteered the bark of the commonwealth

through the troubled feas of the beginning of the queen's reign. No words could better exprefs the habitual thoughtfulnefs, and quiet and dignified courtefy acquired by thofe who are converfant with great affairs and fubtle policy. It is fomewhat remarkable that both thefe poems depict unrequited love, the one on the part of the woman, the other on that of the man. If one were difpofed to find autobiographical hints in Shakefpere's poems, one might argue from hence that he had not found woman's love a folace and a comfort.

The fonnets have always prefented a puzzle to thofe who have endeavoured to draw from them hints with refpect to the Poet's life and fentiments. Some of them, perhaps, may contain allufions to his own circumftances. The following, for inftance, may refer to his profeffion of an actor, then fcarcely freed from the infamy attached to it by the Roman law:—

> " Oh! for my fake do you with fortune chide,
> The guilty goddefs of my harmful deeds,
> That did not better for my life provide
> Than public means, which public manners breeds.
> Thence comes it that my name receives a brand,
> And almoft thence my nature is fubdued
> To what it works in, like the dyer's hand:
> Pity me, then, and wifh I were renewed,
> Whilft, like a willing patient I will drink
> Potions of eyfell 'gainft my ftrong infection;

No bitterness that I will bitter think,
Nor double penance to correct correction.
   Pity me, then, dear friends, and I assure ye
   Even that your pity is enough to cure me."

One of the most beautiful of these exquisite little poems is that in which the Poet laments his friend's absence, or alienation :—

" Full many a glorious morning have I seen
Flatter the mountain-tops with sovereign eye,
Kissing with golden face the meadows green,
Gilding pale streams with heavenly alchemy,
Anon permit the basest clouds to ride
With ugly rack on his celestial face,
And from the forlorn world his visage hide,
Stealing unseen to west with this disgrace :
Even so my sun one early morn did shine,
With all triumphant splendour on my brow,
But, out alack ! he was but one hour mine,
The region cloud hath masked him from me now.
   Yet him for this my love no whit disdaineth ;
   Suns of the world may stain when heaven's sun staineth."

" Stain," in the last line, is a neuter verb. " Heavenly alchemy"—heaven's own art of transmuting baser things to gold—is one of those happy metaphors which denote a true poet.

The dedication prefixed to these sonnets has long been a puzzle to Shakesperian biographers. In the original edition it is not pointed, but in modern editions it has always been printed thus :—

DEDICATION.
TO THE ONLY BEGETTER
OF THESE ENSUING SONNETS,
Mᴿ. W. H.,
ALL HAPPINESS
AND THAT ETERNITY PROMISED
BY OUR EVERLASTING POET,
WISHETH THE
WELL-WISHING ADVENTURER
IN SETTING FORTH,
T. T.

"Mr. W. H.," then, was fuppofed to be "the only begetter" of the fonnets, and no one could make out who "Mr. W. H.," to ₂whom fo high an honour is attributed, was.   Another reading has been fuggefted lately.   A full ftop is placed at "wifheth," to which verb "Mr. W. H." then becomes the nominative cafe, and "T. T.," Thomas Thorpe, the bookfeller, is made merely to defcribe himfelf as "the well-wifhing adventurer in fetting forth."   Point it as we will, however, the dedication, like the fonnets themfelves, remains an enigma which no Œdipus has yet been found to folve.

The lateft attempt which I have feen to trace in the fonnets the Poet's autobiography, is that of Mr. Francis Victor Hugo.   By reading them over frequently, he thinks he has difcovered the real fequence in which they fhould be placed, and arranges them accordingly, introducing fome pieces from "The Paffionate Pilgrim;" and in an "Introduction" explains

the purport of the ftory which he thus makes them
tell. In the firft three fonnets, according to his ar-
rangement, Shakefpere appears in love, and addreffes
his miftrefs in the ufual language of lovers; but fhe
favours another, and in the eighth fonnet the Poet
changes his tone and threatens to go mad and fpeak ill
of her. In the fucceeding fonnets, he accordingly
tells her that he has overrated her beauty, and over-
whelms her with farcafm. She retaliates by re-
minding him that he is married, and therefore, in
loving her, perjured. He retorts, in the twenty-firft
fonnet, that fhe is as much to blame as he; and fhe at
length yields, and the twenty-fifth fonnet is his fong of
triumph. But fhe revenges herfelf, not only by being
unfaithful, but by making his bofom friend, who is
none other than Southampton, his rival. The friend
confeffes his fault, and the Poet "generoufly," as
Mr. Hugo fays, forgives him. The warmth of the
language of the fucceeding fonnets, addreffed to this
faithlefs friend, is explained thus : " Deceived in love
Shakefpere throws himfelf unrefervedly into friendfhip.
From friendfhip he afks that impoffible happinefs
which he has fought elfewhere in vain. From thence-
forth he renounces material affection which is change-
able like the inftincts of animals ; what he feeks
is a love which fhall be immovable, inexhauftible,

ideal. By one of thofe fudden reactions fo frequent
in impetuous natures, he paffes at once from one
extreme to the other, and from having been enfnared
by a courtezan, he attaches himfelf to a foul; in de-
fpair at having been feduced by earthly paffion, he
determines now to love by the intellect alone."

But in reply to this theory it may be afked, Why,
then, were the fonnets difplaced from their natural
order and thereby rendered unintelligible? They were
publifhed in 1609, during the writer's life, and not,
like the plays, after his death; he could, therefore,
have placed them in their proper order.

The myftery is thus explained. Queen Elizabeth,
like *Ferdinand* in "Love's Labour's Loft," had not
only determined herfelf to lead a fingle life, but had
forbidden all her courtiers to marry, and Southampton
among the reft. He, however, yielding to the charms
of "la belle Miftrefs Varnon," and to the eloquent
pleadings of his friend, married, and the confequence
was that he was fent, not for his fuppofed participation
in the attempt of Effex, but for his difobedience to the
Queen's command, to "contemplate the honeymoon
in the Tower of London." The publifhers were, of
courfe, afraid to publifh the fonnets which had been
the caufe of fuch dire evils, during the Queen's life-
time; and when at laft they were given to the world

in the reign of her fucceffor, it was thought convenient
to difguife the name of Southampton under the
initials " W. H.," and the true purport of the fonnets
by deftroying their natural fequence.

The ingenuity of this theory is undeniable, and
Mr. Francis Victor Hugo's little book is well worth
reading; but it muft, of courfe, remain a theory only;
and the latter part, at leaft, relating to Elizabeth and
her decree againft marriage, is fanciful and utterly
without foundation.

Amongft Shakefpere's early productions may be
claffed the fhort poems called "A Lover's Complaint," and "The Paffionate Pilgrim." They contain many pretty paffages, and, in common with his
other poems, are only not fo much thought of and
read becaufe of the overwhelming fplendour of his
dramatic works.

Thefe feveral poems were but the firft effays of
Shakefpere's genius, yet upon them his fame refted
amongft his contemporaries long after fome of his
beft plays had been acted. In the firft ten years
the "Venus and Adonis" paffed through thirteen
editions, while "Romeo and Juliet" was only once
printed.

The fonnet had been introduced from Italy, by Lord
Surrey and Sir Thomas Wyatt, in the reign of Henry

the Eighth. In Italy, Petrarch had invented, or, at leaft, brought it to the higheft perfection of which it is capable; but, like caviar and olives, it is rather a fort of intellectual relifh for thofe whofe palates require a ftimulant, than food fuch as ordinary minds can confume in any quantity. Sonnets muft be read and mufed upon one at a time. A fonnet is founded upon one thought which permeates the complicated metre, and is turned infide out by the metaphyfical ingenuity of the poet. So artificial a ftructure can hardly exprefs ftrong paffion, nor does it convey pleafure to any but thofe who can regard it as a work of art, and follow and appreciate the poet's ingenuity. Its condenfed form always makes it difficult to underftand, and it is only educated minds which take pleafure in the intellectual effort neceffary for the tafk. The age of Elizabeth was a metaphyfical age. The old philofophy and theology ftill influenced men's minds, and prepared them to look for metaphyfics even in poetry. And the conclufion that moft people come to after reading Shakefpere's fonnets is, that they are poetical and intellectual exercifes, not intended to exprefs the Poet's real fentiments, but merely to fhow his fkill in finding poetical thoughts, and drefling them up in poetical language. They entitle him to a place among the metaphyfical poets, Surrey, Wyatt, Ben

Jonfon, Donne, and Cowley, and, I think, they place him at the head of them.

A better preparation for the great dramatic works which were ftill lying unhewn in Shakefpere's brain could hardly have been found than thefe hundred and fifty-four fonnets. In maftering fo thoroughly the difficulties of the metre and of the condenfation of thought and language neceffary in the fonnet, he muft have acquired a facility of writing and power over words which would make them ever afterwards his flaves, and not, as is the cafe with inferior writers and thinkers, his mafters. And this explains the fact, other-wife not the leaft wonderful of the many wonders of his genius, that he never blotted out a word or a line; that the "Hamlet," the "Macbeth," the "Lear," which have exercifed the wits of critics any time this hundred years to fathom the depths of their meaning, flowed fpontaneoufly from his pen, without effort and without hefitation.

A paffage from Mr. Francis Victor Hugo's book, which I have feen fince writing the above, exactly expreffes my idea:—" Englifh, that obftinate jargon [no more a 'jargon' than French, Mr. Hugo!], fo unamenable to rhyme, fo briftling with confonants, Shakefpere undertakes to throw into the crucible of the fonnet, and to draw from thence a language

warm, fparkling, harmonious, all chifeled with anti-
thefes and conceits, which fhall be the language of
Romeo and *Juliet*, of *Othello* and *Defdemona.*"

But the popularity of his early poems was of in-
finite advantage to him, in giving him opportunities of
obferving a phafe of manners with which he could
otherwife fcarcely have become acquainted. It is fomething little fhort of miraculous how Shakefpere, the fon
of a Warwickfhire yeoman, who had never even been at
the Univerfity, fhould have known how to portray men
and women of rank, not only in their graver hours, but
in the eafe and abandonment of focial intercourfe. The
former he might have learnt from books, or from being
prefent at great ftate folemnities, but the latter he could
have known only from taking part in it. The dialogues
between *Prince Henry* and *Poyns* and *Falftaff*, between
Romeo, Mercutio, and *Benvolio*, between *Rofalind, Celia,*
and *Orlando,* and between *Beatrice* and *Benedict*, are
of the very beft ftyle of wellbred converfation. It is
fufficiently wonderful how, under any circumftances,
he could have fo accurately caught the tone of good
fociety. We fee daily how very indifferently even
clever novelifts, who have lived amongft fafhionable
people all their lives, depict their manners. Shakefpere, of courfe, could not have attained this excellence
by fimple intuition. He muft have fomewhere feen the

original from which he drew. I think it is probable, therefore, that his early poems were the means of introducing him to the fociety of people of refinement and high breeding, whofe manners his extraordinary powers of perception enabled him fo accurately to obferve and reproduce. And thus, I think, the poems, and the fame they brought him, may have combined to prepare Shakefpere for the great dramatic career which his father's misfortunes and his own were the means of opening to him in London.

CHAPTER IX.

SHAKESPERE was one of thofe men who have got a great deal into a fhort life. Before he had attained the age of thirty he had fown fome very wild oats at Stratford, and got into confiderable trouble; he had managed his love-making and matrimonial affairs in fuch a way as not by any means to fmooth his way out of his difficulties; he had gone to London a ruined man, with a very flender education, and had adopted the firft menial office which promifed him bread; but by the time that he was thirty, he found himfelf eftablifhed amongft the foremoft poets of a poetic age, gaining a handfome competence as author, actor, and fhareholder in the Globe and Blackfriars theatres, the envy of his profligate and unhappy fellow-dra-matifts, like Green, and the friend of men of rank and refinement, like Southampton.

But while all thefe honours and emoluments were flowing in upon him in London, he ftill confidered

the little village in Warwickfhire where he was born
as his real home. Aubrey fays that he " was wont to
goe to his native countreye once a yeare;" and there is
a tradition that on thefe occafions he ufed to take up
his quarters at the Crown inn, near Carfax, at Oxford.
The houfe is now divided into fhops, but retains much
of its ancient chara&ter. It was kept by one Davenant,
father of Sir William Davenant, the dramatift, in con-
ne&tion with whom a fcandalous ftory was in circula-
tion, after the Reftoration, refpe&ting the Poet; but as
it is grounded upon no tangible evidence I do not care
to record it. At Stratford it is probable he left his
wife and family during his early ftruggles, and we may
fancy how refrefhing it muft have been to the country-
loving Poet to revifit every year the fcenes of his early
adventures, and to fee his young family growing up,
while he felt that he was every year increafing his
means of providing for them. A family merrymaking,
at which the Combes, Hathaways, Halls, Ardens, would
meet over a bowl of lambfwool, was in his eyes better
than the wit-combats at the " Mermaid." With what
delight muft he have feen the Avon flowing majefti-
cally at the foot of the town by the fine old church!
How pleafant muft have appeared to him the glades
and groves of Charlecote and Fulbrooke after the
" melancholy of Houndfditch!" And how fweet muft

have founded to him the cry of the hounds in the woodlands of Arden. Probably quite as sweet as the plaudits of the theatre.

Indeed, one of the most curious traits of his character was his love for an unambitious country life in his native town. Like another of the world's great poets, he really might say—

" Flumina amem sylvasque inglorius."

He seems to have looked upon his literary fame only as a means to enable him to retire honourably to Stratford; and he was content that to be the author of " Hamlet," " Lear," " The Tempest," " As You Like It," and the rest of those great works which will last out the English language, should bring him no higher reward than might have been gained by a career of successful farming or trade.

This is a very English feeling. Horace Walpole was rather ashamed of being a literary man; Walter Scott was much prouder of being the Laird of Abbotsford than the author of " Waverley;" and I fancy that Mr. Anthony Trollope, when got up in his " pink " and " tops," and standing by a covert in the Rodings waiting for a fox to be found, would consider it very bad taste for any one to allude to " The Small House at Allington." A foreigner cannot understand this

feeling. If, by writing a clever *feuilleton* in a paper he
has obtained the croſs of the Legion of Honour, he
will wear the ribbon in the button-hole of his ſhooting-
jacket; indeed it is not clear to me that he does not
wear it in his night-ſhirt. We, on the contrary, think
literature a ſort of occupation which rather unfits a man
for the buſineſs of the world, and look upon a literary
man with ſome degree of ſuſpicion and diſtruſt; and
moſt Engliſhmen would rather derive an hereditary
fortune from a county magiſtrate, who had juſt brains
enough to adjudicate on a poaching caſe with the
aſſiſtance of a clerk, than from having written "Waverley," or "Pickwick."

In his careleſſneſs of literary fame, Shakeſpere was
true to the national character. He reminds one of thoſe
people in Chaucer's "Houſe of Fame," who cared not
for renown :—

> " With that, about I clewed mine head,
>   And ſaw anon the fifth rout,
>   That to this lady [Fame] gan to lout,
>   And down on knees anon to fall;
>   And to her then beſoughten all
>   To hiden their good workès eke,
>   And ſaid they would not give a leek
>   For no fame, nor for ſuch renown.
>
>   *   *   *   *   *
>
>   ' What ?' quoth ſhe, ' and be ye wood? [mad]
>   And ween ye for to doen good,

And for to have of that no fame ?
Have ye defpite to have my name ?
Nay, ye fhall lyen every one !
Blow up thy trump, and that anon,'
Quoth fhe, ' thou Eolus yhote,
 [Thou who art called Eolus]
And ring thefe folkès works by note,
That all the world may of it hear.' "

We fhould have expected that Shakefpere would
have fettled in London, to be near his great friends, to
mix with the wits, and take his accuftomed chair in
the evening at fome club of chofen fpirits, like Dryden,
Addifon, and Johnfon, and pronounce, *ex cathedrâ*,
upon the merits of the lateft play. But inftead of
this, the firftfruits of his profperity are feen in his
endeavour to eftablifh himfelf in a good pofition in his
native town. In 1597 his parents, John and Mary
Shakefpere, filed a bill in Chancery for the recovery of
the eftate of Afhbies, which they had mortgaged, and
of which the mortgage was alleged to have been fore-
clofed. Now, a Chancery fuit is not a cheap luxury,
and it is not likely that John Shakefpere, the poor
bankrupt of a few years back, fhould fo foon have
retrieved his affairs as to be able to indulge in it.
There was then no Commiffioner of Bankrupts to
wipe out an unlucky tradefman's liabilities, and enable
him to ftart afrefh and make a fortune as if nothing
had happened. The renowned cafe of " Bardwell

againſt Pickwick" had not yet been publiſhed to the world, and debtors, once in priſon, were there till death releaſed them. To Shakeſpere himſelf, then, we muſt attribute this attempt to reſcue his mother's patrimony from the mortgageor. It was the proceeds of the ſale of the poems, and ſuch plays as he had then written, and the profits of the Globe and Blackfriars, that went to fee the Chancery lawyers for their unſuccefsful attempt to keep Aſhbies in the family.

To the ſame defire to aſſume a poſition among the gentlemen of his county may be aſſigned his father's application to the Heralds' Office about the ſame time for a grant of arms; this, however, was not iſſued till 1599. It recites that John Shakeſpere's " parent, great-grandfather, and late anteceſſor, for his faithful and approved ſervice to the late moſt prudent prince, King Henry the Seventh, of famous memorie, was advaunced and rewarded with lands and tenements, given to him in thoſe parts of Warwickſhire where they have continewed by ſome defcents in good repu-tation and credit; and for that the ſaid John Shak-ſpeare having marryed the daughter and one of the heyrs of Robert Arden, of Wellingcote, in the ſaid countie, and alſo produced this his auncient cote-of-arms, heretobefore aſſigned to him whileſt he was her Majeſtie's officer and baylefe of that towne : in con-

fideration of the premiſſes and for the encouragement
of his poſteritie, unto whome ſuch blazon of arms and
achievements of inheritance from theyre ſaid mother
by the auncyent cuſtom and laws of arms maye law-
fully defend : we the ſaid Garter and Clarencieulx have
aſſigned, graunted, and by theſe preſents exempleſied
unto the ſaid John Shakſpeare, and to his poſteritie,
that ſhield and cote-of-arms, viz., In a field of gould
upon a bend, ſables, a ſpeare of the firſt, the poynt
upward, hedded argent; and for his creſt or cognizance,
A falcon with his wings deſplayed, ſtanding on a wrethe
of his coullers, ſupporting a ſpeare armed, hedded, or
ſteeled, ſilver, fixed upon a helmet with mantell and
taſſels, &c."

In the original draft of the grant by Dethick, and
in ſeveral other documents, I find the name ſpelt
" Shakeſpere," which ſpelling I follow for the following
reaſons—the College of Arms is the beſt authority
in the matter of names; the name is an old one in
Warwickſhire, and the correct ſpelling of the two
words of which it is compoſed is "ſhake" and "ſpere."
In the reign of Elizabeth an " a " was introduced into
ſuch words as were originally ſpelt with an " e " alone
—as ſpear, head, ſtead, mead, fear; for ſpere, hede,
ſtede, mede, fere—to the great detriment of the language; and in the name Shakeſpere I ſee no reaſon to

adopt it. The name is fpelt in numerous different ways even by Shakefpere himfelf, and I adopt that which was the mode of fpelling it when it was firft adopted by his anceftors.

In 1597 the wifhed-for opportunity of fecuring a place of retirement in his native town occurred. New Place, the beft houfe in Stratford, was for fale, and Shakefpere bought it for the fum of fixty pounds. It had been built in the reign of Henry the Seventh by the magnificent Sir Hugh Clopton, the builder of the bridge and reftorer of the chapel, directly oppofite to which it ftood. It is thus defcribed by Dugdale :—
" On the north fide of this chapel was a fair houfe, built of brick and timber by the faid Sir Hugh, wherein he lived in his latter days and died." Sir Hugh bequeathed it to William Clopton, of Clopton, from whom it paffed to William Bott. Its next pof-feffor was William Underhill, of Eatington and Idli-cote, from whom Shakefpere bought it in Eafter term, 1597. In the conveyance it is defcribed in the comical dog-Latin of the law, to confift " de uno mefuagio, duobus horreis, duobus gardinis cum per-tinentiis " (of one meffuage, two barns, and two gar-dens, with their appurtenances). There is no draw-ing of it extant, for the pretended one publifhed by Malone is a palpable forgery. That it was a com-

fortable, and even ftately refidence, may be inferred
from the faƈt that it was built by Sir Hugh Clopton,
that it was the beft houfe in the town, and that when
Queen Henrietta Maria afterwards fojourned for a
while at Stratford, fhe took up her abode there. On
Shakefpere's death, in default of heirs male of his
daughters, Sufanna and Judith, it defcended to his
right heirs, that is to fay, to the daughter of Sufanna
Hall, married to Thomas Nafh, and afterwards to
Sir John Barnard. She died without iffue, and New
Place was fold to Sir Hugh Clopton, a defcendant of
the original builder, who almoft entirely pulled it down
and rebuilt it. After Sir Hugh's death his houfe was
fold to the Rev. Francis Gaftrell. This gentleman,
who was married to a friend and correfpondent of
Dr. Johnfon, confidering that it was rated too highly
to the relief of the poor, pulled down the houfe in 1757,
having firft cut down a fine mulberry-tree which was
faid to have been planted by Shakefpere's own hands
in the gardens. The caufe alleged for this felfifh aƈt
was, that the reverend gentleman, who appears to have
been an epicure, and fond of his eafe, was annoyed by
the flux of company who came to vifit the interefting
relic. Upon the old foundations was built a modern
houfe, which, having been purchafed for the public
within the laft few years, was pulled down, in the

hope that fome remains of that in which Shakefpere lived might be difcovered.

When I vifited it, it prefented a moft forlorn and miferable appearance. Nothing was to be feen but a newly-made garden, and the rubbifh and foundations of a houfe. The only parts remaining of the original building in which Shakefpere lived are the ftone foundations of the main wall, abutting on Chapel Lane, a portion of the porch wall, and a well, from which were taken a candleftick, knife, tobacco-pipes, tiles, glafs, and fome pieces of iron. The further fide of the plot of ground is bounded by a fhed, which is dignified by the name of "The Theatre." Had the old houfe, where Shakefpere fpent the laft years of his life in eafe and opulence, furrounded by his family, and where fome of his greateft works were written, remained, it would really have been a relic of intereft; but the place has been thoroughly and effectually denuded of everything upon which it is poffible to fix any affociation with Shakefpere. The little piece of ftone wall which formed the foundation of the houfe tells no intelligible tale of the illuftrious inhabitant. Still there at leaft is the ground upon which he walked, and the garden which he probably took pleafure in cultivating, and it is well to keep up our veneration for genius by refpect for the place confecrated by being the fcene of fome of its happieft creations. " Far from me and from my friends," fays Dr. Johnfon, " be fuch frigid philofophy as may conduct us indifferent and unmoved over any ground which has been dignified by wifdom, bravery, or virtue. That man is little to be envied whofe patriotifm would not gain force upon the plain of Marathon, or whofe piety would not grow warmer among the ruins of Iona ;" or, we may add, whofe veneration for genius would not grow deeper among the remains of Shakefpere's home.

Mr. Edwards' photograph gives the little bit of the foundation of the porch and the boundary wall, with the theatre in the background. The reader will fee that it is a fcene of moft admired dif- order, and what fhape it will ultimately affume I know not.

The mulberry-tree, cut down by Mr. Gaftrell and his wife, was fold for fire-wood, and bought by a Mr. Thomas Sharp, a watch-maker in the town, who cut it up and made it into various little knick-knacks, which were greedily purchafed by admirers of the Poet. Mifs Burdett Coutts poffeffes a chair made of it, with a medallion in the back, carved by Hogarth ; and the cup from which Garrick drank when he fang the foolifh fong compofed for the Shakefpere jubilee, was alfo made of it. Mr. W. O. Hunt, the donor of

the portrait now to be feen in the houfe in Henley Street, has a table made of the fame wood.

The veneration paid to thefe trifling remains fhows how naturally we affociate the work of art with the artift. The plays would have the fame excellence by whomfoever they might have been written. There is no intrinfic connection between them and the man William Shakefpere. He has been long dead, and they remain a poffeffion for ever. But the mind refufes to view things from this abftract and cold point of view. It infifts upon tracing the work to the workman, and connects by fome wayward and irrational, but ftill natural procefs, " Lear," " Hamlet," and the reft of thofe wondrous poems, with a cup or a fnuff-box made of a piece of mulberry-tree !

CHAPTER X.

COCKNEYISM is one of the old inftitutions of the country which railroads have done much to modify. There was a time when barrifters and attorneys ufed to live all the year round, to eat, drink, fleep, and keep their carriages, in the gloomy ftreets near the Old Bailey and Weftminfter Hall. Indeed, perfons now alive can recollect an eminent civilian who had a handfome houfe and eftablifhment in Doctors' Commons, and never thought of leaving it. Publifhers not only had their warehoufes, but lived in Paternofter Row; tradefmen in Cheapfide, winter and fummer. Grub Street was the chofen abode of authors. Johnfon lived in Bolt Court, and thought the view down Fleet Street the fineft profpect in England. The country was confidered a fort of wildernefs, and a chance vifit to fome remote county was fufficient occafion for writing a book about fhepherds and fhepherdeffes. London was the centre of intelligence, and he who was not up to all its ways—who did not know the fafhionable taverns, and could not call the waiters at them by their Chriftian names—was called a gull and a ninny.

Railroads have changed all this. Lawyers, bankers, tradefmen, and innkeepers, and even publifhers and authors, now live ten, twenty, or thirty miles from town, in a country houfe with a demefne and farm attached to it, where they fpend, upon growing grapes and pines, turnips and mangold wurtzel, prize beef and mutton, pheafants and partridges, the money which has been fpun from their brains, or abftracted from their clients' or cuftomers' pockets in a gloomy den in the City. A friend and neighbour of mine, an eminent lawyer, who is no lefs remarkable for his legal acumen than for his fkill as a fportfman, and who in the very whirlwind of his practice has always given two days a-week to fhooting or fifhing, was complaining one day to the farmer who fupplied him with corn for his pheafants, of the quantity of barley which appeared againft him in his bill. "Ah!" fays Hodge, "you don't mind a quarter or two o' barley more or lefs in a half-year! *You'll* make it all right when you git a robbin' on 'em up in Lonon!" And Hodge was right. You pafs an exquifitely kept place which puts the old fquire's quite to the blufh, and you are told that it belongs to the grocer in Piccadillywhere you got a jar of ginger the

T

day before. You fee a man perfectly got up in pink and
leathers and tops, fplendidly mounted and followed by
a groom on his fecond horfe, and what is more, riding
well to hounds; all this is derived from the calico ware-
houfe in Cheapfide, or from the magazine of "leading
articles" in Printing Houfe Square. A pack of harriers
dafh acrofs the road followed by a gentleman in green;
this gallant fportfman is the eminent publifher who
thus learns whether to accept or refufe the MS. of
Mr. St. Hubert's fporting novel. And to go a ftep
lower in the focial fcale—whofe is this neat little villa
with its fmall coach-houfe and ftable, and little paddock
in which grazes a pretty Alderney cow? That is
Mr. Whiff's, the tobacconift, in the Strand. All this
is the falutary effect of railroads, which enable men of
bufinefs to fleep in the pure air of the country, and be
at their fhops or offices by bufinefs hours in the morning; which gives them healthful and civilifing amufements for their leifure hours, and infures health and
vigour to their children. I don't mean to fay that this
double life wholly eradicates the inftincts, language,
and manners, which ufed to mark the dwellers within
the found of Bow-bells, or that the profufe magnifi-
cence of a Londoner's eftablifhment in the country is
as pleafing as the fimpler ftyle of the old fquire's—
that would be too much to expect; but ftill the more

falient angles of Cockneyifm have been rubbed off; and what is more, thofe whofe taftes and habits lead them to prefer a country life can now, by means of the railroad, participate in fome degree in the pecuniary advantages of the great market, where a purchafer may be found for any article, whether manufactured by the hands or created by the brain.

Shakefpere lived before Watt had invented the fteam-engine, or Stephenfon had applied it to locomotion; but he anticipated in fome degree the dual life which it enables us now to lead. London was never his real home—Stratford was the home of his mind. In the very hey-day of his fame and profperity the little village on the Avon, with its fimple fociety of country fquires and yeomen, its farming and field fports, was the object towards which his life pointed; and to this, I think, we owe the healthy tone of his great dramatic poems and their variety of intereft. Compare them with the plays of Jonfon, Greene, Peele, and Marlowe, Beaumont and Fletcher, Dryden, Wycherley, and Congreve, and one of the marks by which they are diftinguifhed, and their chiefeft charm, will be found to be the fuperior reality of the pictures of country life and character which they prefent. The town fupplies but few phafes of character; but Shakefpere had the whole range at his command. While mixing in all the humours of the court and city, his yearly vifits to his native village kept his mind frefh and fweet, and enabled it to work amidft the reek of the theatres and taverns of the city without being tainted or enfeebled.

As a pilgrim to Stratford, I ought, perhaps, to confine myfelf entirely to his doings in his country home; but, I think, we can hardly judge what manner of man he was without a glance at the other life he led in London.

In the firft place it was a life of labour. We have feen that before 1598 he had written his poems, and either retouched or written fifteen or fixteen plays, amongft which are fome of his beft, fuch as "The Merchant of Venice," "A Midfummer Night's Dream," "Romeo and Juliet," and "Henry the Fourth," Part I. It is impoffible, after this, to determine exactly the year in which each play was produced, but from internal and external evidence, Malone, Mr. Halliwell, Mr. Dyce, and others, have arrived at an approximation to it. They all agree generally to attribute to the year 1599, "Much Ado about Nothing" and "Henry the Fifth;" to 1600, "As You Like It" and "The Moor of Venice;" to 1601, "The Merry Wives of Windfor" and "King Henry the Eighth;" to 1602, "Twelfth Night" and "Hamlet;" to 1603, "Meafure for Meafure" and "Julius Cæfar;" to 1605,

" Lear " and " Macbeth ;" to 1607 and 1608, " Anthony and Cleopatra " and " Troilus and Creffida ;"
to 1609, " Cymbeline ;" to 1610, " Coriolanus " and
" Timon of Athens ;" to 1611, " A Winter's Tale "
and " The Tempeft," the moft perfect as a work of art
of all his dramatic poems. Like *Profpero*, he is fuppofed, with this crowning exercife of his magic power, to
have laid by his conjuring robe and wand. Within the
fpace of nineteen years, therefore, he muft have written
thirty-one plays at leaft, befides retouching others, fuch
as " Pericles," " Titus Andronicus," and the three parts
of " Henry the Sixth," and taking part in the general
theatrical bufinefs of the Globe and the theatre at the
Blackfriars.

It is curious to obferve what a deep abyfs of ignorance lies beneath the knowledge which is now-a-days
fpread over fo large a furface. It reminds one of thofe
beautifully green fpots of herbage which appear to
offer fafe footing on the banks of a fluggifh ftream, but
as foon as your horfe treads upon them the upper cruft
of verdure gives way, and you find yourfelf plunging
helplefsly up to the girths in black mud. Of the many
people who talk of Shakefpere, how many have read
all his plays? Of the felect few who have read his
plays, how many have tried to form a conception of
the mode of their conftruction? And yet what a lazy,

incurious mind muſt that be which can go on contem-
plating a phenomenon which is almoſt miraculous,
and never ſeeking to penetrate the myſtery! It is as
if a man were daily to ſee the bones and tuſks of the
maſtodon and the ichthyoſaurus, the ſtems of giant
ferns, and the ſhells of unknown molluſcs, thrown up
by the pick of the quarryman, and ſhould never inquire
how the earth was made. I muſt confeſs, with ſhame,
that long after I had learned to read Shakeſpere with
ſome degree of diſcrimination, and to appreciate his
ſuperiority to any other dramatic poet I had read, I
was content to accept the fa&t that the plays had been
written by an uneducated man in the reign of Queen
Elizabeth, without further inquiry. As far as I thought
about the matter, I believed that he had produced the
whole thing, plots and all, by a ſort of plenary inſpira-
tion, or by the help of a meſſenger from above, like
Numa's Egeria, or Mahomet's pigeon. And I ſuppoſe
a great many of thoſe who really more or leſs enjoy
ſuch plays as "The Tempeſt," and "A Midſummer
Night's Dream," and "As You Like It," are in the
ſame ſtate of happy ignorance. Shakeſpere's genius
can hardly be overrated, but yet it was not equal to ſuch
a ſtupendous effort as this.

There is ſcarcely one of the plays of which the plot
may not be traced to ſome previous writer. But is

Shakefpere to be accufed of plagiarifm or want of invention for this? Certainly not. The object of a play is not to tell a ftory, but to fhow men and women acting under the influence of ftrong paffion. And, therefore, Horace, in the Epiftle to the Pifos, de arte poeticà, properly advifes authors to choofe fome fable well known to the audience, fo that he may take them with him at once into the very midft of the action. It detracts nothing from the merits of the hiftorical plays that the incidents are taken bodily from North's "Plutarch," Holinfhed, or Geoffrey of Monmouth; becaufe it is not the proper bufinefs of the dramatift to invent plots, but rather to reprefent character in action. Geoffrey may tell us that *Lear* went mad, but who but Shakefpere could have imagined the fcene in the hut where the old king arraigns *Goneril* and *Regan*, while the *Fool* heightens the reality and the pathos of the circum-ftance by his comments, and *Edgar* enhances the difmal horror of it by his fnatches of "Tom o' Bedlam" fongs? Holinfhed may tell how Harry, Prince of Wales, forgot his ftation for a time to haunt taverns with loofe companions; but it was referved for Shake-fpere to imagine the wit and fun which tempted him to leave his fphere. Nor even in the romantic plays was the dramatift bound to invent his own plots, when he could find them ready made in Boccaccio's "Deca-meron." The Italian novelift relates the incidents fo terfely that they have almoft the air of being the arguments of a poem. They are the very fkeletons which Shakefpere, and before him Chaucer, clothed with flefh and blood. Sir Edward Bulwer Lytton's "Eugene Aram" is not the lefs an original novel for being founded on fact, nor is Mr. Dickens's "Oliver Twift," becaufe he had probably learned many of the incidents at the police courts.

Such has been the induftry of Shakefperian critics that the plots of almoft all the plays have been traced to their fources. To take them in the approximate order of their compofition rather than in that in which they were printed in the firft complete edition, which is the folio of 1623, and which is followed in modern editions—the three parts of "Henry the Sixth" can fcarcely be called Shakefpere's. They are, in fact, Marlowe's plays, retouched by him. The "Comedy of Errors" was probably taken from a play founded on the "Menæchmi" of Plautus, acted before Queen Eliza-beth, at Hampton Court, on New Year's Day, at night, "by the children of Pawles," that is, the choir boys. The ftory of "Love's Labour 's Loft" has been traced by Mr. Dyce to an incident related in Monftrelet's "Chronicle." The incident of the cafkets in "The

Merchant of Venice " is found in Gower's " Confeffio
Amantis," and that relating to the Jew in the " Gefta
Romanorum," as alfo in a ballad publifhed by Percy.
For the incidents of " Richard the Second," Shakefpere
was indebted to an older play or to the Chronicles.
The " Two Gentlemen of Verona " is founded on an
older play called " The Hiftory of Felix and Philif-
mena," played before Queen Elizabeth in 1584. " A
Midfummer Night's Dream " appears to be one of the
moft original of the plays. The plot is found in no
previous work as yet difcovered, but the materials for
the feparate parts may have been derived by Shakefpere from North's " Plutarch" and Ovid's " Metamor-
phofes." *Oberon, Titania, Puck,* and the other ouphes,
are the genuine growth of the popular Englifh imagination, and Shakefpere probably drew his conception
of them from the tales he had heard by the firefide
on winter evenings in the farmhoufes of Warwickfhire. " The Taming of a Shrew " is a recaft of a
play " at fundry times acted by the Right Honorable
the Earle of Pembrook his fervants." " Romeo and
Juliet" is " The Tragicall Hiftorye of Romeus and
Juliet, written firft in Italian by Bandell, and now in
Englifh by Arthur Brooke" (1562), dramatifed. "Henry
the Fourth," Parts I and II., and " Henry the Fifth,"
are founded upon older plays. *Sir John Falftaff,* in

Shakefpere's firft draught called *Sir John Oldcaftle*, is, of courfe, the undivided property of the great mafter. He was no doubt as great a favourite of Shakefpere's as Sir Roger de Coverley was of Addifon's. Shakefpere cannot part with him. He takes him through the two parts of "Henry the Fourth," "Henry the Fifth," and "The Merry Wives of Windfor," and is careful to make his death as unexpectedy tragical as the nature of the cafe would admit. He knew that the foil which could throw up fuch a luxuriant crop of wit muft have been deep and rich by nature. The tattle of *Quickly* and the *Page*, as they tell the ghaftly ftory of his deathbed, gives us a glimpfe of the ftruggle between *Falftaff's* better nature and early recollections, and his long habits of debauchery. This was a touch of nature which none but the mafter could throw in. "Richard the Third" is founded upon hiftory alone, though there was a former play on the fame fubject. "All's Well that Ends Well" is from the "Deca-meron" of Boccaccio, and is, indeed, thoroughly Italian in its plot. "King John" is founded upon an earlier anonymous play. "Much Ado about Nothing" is founded remotely on a ftory in Bandello. The general plot of "As You Like It" is to be found in "The Cokes Tale of Gamelyn," generally included in Chaucer's Canterbury Tales, but not, I think, written by Chaucer.

"The Moor of Venice" is from a ſtory in Cinthio's
"Heccatommithi." The ſtories of "Hamlet," "Lear,"
and "Macbeth," were popular in chronicles and hiſ-
tories in Shakeſpere's time. "Julius Cæſar," "Anthony and Cleopatra," and "Coriolanus," are taken
from North's "Plutarch." The original of "Timon
of Athens" is in Lucian, but the ſtory of the Miſan-
thrope was current in the ſixteenth century. Shakeſpere might have got all the incidents of "Troilus and
Creſſida" from Chaucer's exquiſite love-ſtory, itſelf a
recaſt of Boccaccio's "Filoſtrato," but he has given a
totally different reading of the characters. I ſuppoſe I
ſhall be accuſed of rank hereſy, but I muſt acknowledge that I prefer Chaucer's poem to Shakeſpere's
play. The play is to me the only unpleaſing one of
Shakeſpere's; the poem is one of the moſt elaborately
beautiful in the Engliſh, or indeed in any, language,
and far ſuperior to Boccaccio's. The remote original
of "Cymbeline" is a very ancient romance, publiſhed
by M. Franciſque Michel in his "Théâtre Français du
Moyen-Age," from which is taken the "Roman de
Violette;" but whether Shakeſpere borrowed his plot
from either of theſe, or from ſome Engliſh tranſlation,
I cannot tell. The ſtory was extant, at any rate, long
before his time. "A Winter's Tale" is dramatiſed
from Greene's novel, called "Pandoſto;" but as yet no

original has been found for Shakefpere's moft perfect
and finifhed work, "The Tempeft." Defert iflands,
magicians, fpirits of air and water, damfels who had
never feen a man, abound in the literature of romance;
but I am glad to believe that Shakefpere is indebted
to no one for the exquifite combination of all thefe
incidents which forms "The Tempeft."

From this furvey it would appear that Shakefpere fet
himfelf, in a bufinefs-like way, to provide plays for the
theatre in which he had a fhare, without much regard
to anything but pleafing the public for the moment.
For this purpofe he ranfacked the works of his predeceffors and contemporaries, he read the old chronicles
and romances, he feized upon every Englifh verfion of
an Italian novel as it came out, and for claffical ftories
had recourfe to North's "Plutarch," a tranflation of a
French tranflation. In "The Tempeft" is a whole
paffage taken from Florio's then recently publifhed tranflation of "Montaigne's Effays." A copy, with Shakefpere's autograph, or alleged autograph in it, is now
preferved in the Britifh Mufeum. That he was greedy
of all knowledge there can be no doubt. His mind
muft have been ftored with philofophy, divinity, law,
art; and this varied knowledge, which was quite a
different thing from claffical fcholarfhip, flowed into
his dialogue, and gives it that richnefs which we

scarcely find in any other writer. This was the effect
of his genius; but everything concurs to show that
his immediate object was gained when his plays filled
the house. He never blotted or erased his manuscript.
He took no care to collect his works and publish them
during his life-time, and they were not in fact collected
till nearly ten years after his death.

Now it appears to me, though the proposition
seem paradoxical, that this writing for an immediate
and tangible object was one cause of Shakespere's excellence. He knew that he had the secret of pleasing
the public, and he had no crotchets about writing for
posterity to mar the simplicity of his aim. He was not
oppressed by the greatness of his task, and his thoughts,
therefore, flowed the more freely and effectively. I
think it will be found that works of art produced to
answer some obvious end—paintings painted expressly
to decorate some particular building, like those of
Giotto; histories, compiled to serve some political or
religious purpose, like Gibbon's Decline and Fall and
Macaulay's England; pamphlets to overwhelm some
personal enemy, like the Letters of Junius or Drapier,
or the poem of "Hudibras"—*facit indignatio versus*—
and plays written with the sole purpose of filling the
house, like Shakespere's, are the very works that posterity will not suffer to perish. The great fault of the

later poets, thofe of the lakes in particular, was that they had fome dream of perfection in their head which was too high for common men of their own generation— fome ideal of beauty which ordinary men could not tafte, and they have fo far endangered their permanent fame. Shakefpere, apparently, cared only to pleafe the audience at the Globe and Blackfriars, and he has " built himfelf an everlafting name."

Of his focial life—where he lived, and with whom, when he was in London—little is known, except that he was, as we have feen, noted for the ftraightforward honefty of his dealings and his pleafing manners, and that he was deemed worthy of the fpecial regard of Queen Elizabeth and King James, and of the friend-fhip of Southampton.

His humbler friends were the other poets of his time, among whom Ben Jonfon ftands pre-eminent for his affectionate and judicious praife. The foundation of their friendfhip was laid in an act of kindnefs on Shakefpere's part which a literary man would be likely never to forget. Jonfon, though the fon of a me-chanic, had been brought up at the renowned college of St. Peter's, Weftminfter; for, indeed, the ancient foundations of our great public fchools were intended for the education of poor fcholars. After this he be-came a bricklayer, following the trade of his ftepfather,

and Fuller fays that he "helped in the ftructure of
Lincoln's Inn, when, having a trowel in his hand, he
had a book in his pocket." Scorning fo mechanical
an employment, he went as a foldier to the wars in the
Low Countries, and, returned from thence, took to
literature as a means of living, and while yet quite
unknown, offered his celebrated "Every Man in his
Humour" to the company at the Blackfriars. The
manager failed to tafte the humour of *Bobadil* and *Brain-
worm*, and was about to return the play with one of
thofe difagreeable anfwers with which fome managers
and publifhers are faid to damp the hopes of unknown
authors, when Shakefpere afked to fee it, and was fo
pleafed with it as to procure its acceptance. The acquaintance thus begun was ripened into friendfhip by
frequent focial meetings at the "Mermaid Tavern," in
Bread Street, where Sir Walter Raleigh had founded a
club, the earlieft probably known in England. It is
alluded to by Jonfon in his lines "Inviting a Friend
to Supper "—

> " To-night, grave fir, both my poor houfe and I
>   Do equally defire your company ;
>   Not that we think us worthy fuch a gueft,
>   But that your worth will dignify our feaft
>   With thofe that come ; whofe grace may make that feem
>   Something, which elfe could hope for no efteem.
>   It is the fair acceptance, fir, creates
>   The entertainment perfect, not the cates.

Yet fhall you have, to rectify your palate,
An olive, capers, or fome bitter sallat,
Ufhering the mutton, with a fhort-legged hen,
If we caught her full of eggs, and then
Lemons and wine for fauce ; to thefe a coney,
Is not to be defpaired of for our money;
And though fowl now be fcarce, yet there are clerks,
The fky not falling, think we may have larks.
I'll tell of more, and lie, fo you will come,
Of partridge, pheafant, woodcock, of which fome
May yet be there, and godwit, if we can,
Knot, rail, and ruff, too. Howfoe'er, my man
Shall read a piece of Virgil, Tacitus,
Livy, or of fome better book to us,
Of which we'll fpeak our minds amidft our meat,
And I'll profefs no verfes to repeat.
To this, if aught appear which I not know of,
That will the paftry, not my paper fhow of;
Digeftive cheefe and fruit there fure will be.
But that which moft doth take my mufe and me,
Is a pure cup of rich Canary wine,
Which is the Mermaid's now, but fhall be mine;
Of which had Horace or Anacreon tafted,
Their lives, as do their lines, till now had lafted."

Allufion is again made to this celebrated tavern in
" The Voyage :"—

" It was the day, what time the powerful moon
Makes the poor Bankfide creature wet its fhoon
In its own hall ; when thefe (in worthy fcorn
Of thofe that put out monies on return
From Venice, Paris, or fome inland paffage
Of fix times to and fro, without embaffage,
Or him that backwards went to Berwick, or which
Did dance the famous Morris into Norwich)
At Bread Street's Mermaid having dined, and merry,
Propofed to go to Holborn in a wherry."

I have quoted the former of thefe paffages becaufe it gives a curious infight into the focial cuftoms of Shake- fpere's time. From it we learn that it was not unufual for one to read out fome entertaining book during dinner, as they read out paffages from Scripture, or the " Lives of the Saints," in monafteries. It alfo gives one fome idea of the luxury in which literary men lived, befides fome curious gaftronomical facts, fuch as that olives were eaten before, not after dinner.

At the " Mermaid," then, ufed to meet the wits of the town—Shakefpere, Jonfon, Beaumont, Fletcher, Selden, Donne. And here, as quaint old Fuller in his " Worthies" relates, " Many were the wit combats between him [Shakefpere] and Ben Jonfon, which two I behold like a Spanifh great galleon and an Englifh man-of-war: Mafter Jonfon, like the former, was built higher in learning, folid but flow in his perform- ances; Shakefpere, with the Englifh man-of-war, leffer in bulk, but lighter in failing, could turn with all tides, tack about and take advantage of all winds, by the quicknefs of his wit and invention."

Of this wit the fpecimens which have been preferved do not give a very exalted notion; but it is a curious fact that converfation which has delighted the hearers by its wit, when repeated, often feems infipid. A joke which the reports of the debates in Parliament declare to have been received with roars of "laughter," often feems fo poor and trivial that we think our legiflators muft be wonderfully eafily amufed. Yet they are the moft faftidious audience in the world. The joke was not a bad joke in reality, but wit read is not like wit fpoken. The time, place, and manner have much to do with it. So *Falftaff*, a great authority furely on this fubject, fays, "Oh, it is much that a jeft with a grave face and a flight oath will do with a fellow that hath never had the ache in his fhoulders!" Befides, wit is of fo flight and evanefcent a character that it is not the beft jokes that are remembered, but rather the heavieft and dulleft. Barrow defines wit thus: "Sometimes it lieth in a pat allufion to a known ftory, or in a feafonable application of a trivial faying, or in forging an appofite tale; fometimes it playeth in words and phrafes, taking advantage from the ambiguity of their fenfe, or the affinity of their found; fometimes it is wrapped in a drefs of humorous expreffion; fometimes it lurketh under an odd fimilitude; fometimes it is lodged in a fly queftion, in a fmart anfwer, in a quirkifh reafon, in a fhrewd intimation, in cunningly averting or cleverly retorting an objection; fometimes it is couched in a bold fcheme of fpeech, in a tart irony, in a lufty hyperbole, in a ftartling metaphor, in a plaufible reconciling of contradictions, or in acute nonfenfe; fometimes a fcenical reprefentation of perfons or things, a counterfeit fpeech, a mimical look or gefture, paffeth for it; fometimes an affected fimplicity, fometimes a prefumptuous blunt-nefs giveth it being; fometimes it rifeth only from a lucky hitting upon what is ftrange; fometimes from a crafty wrefting obvious matter to the purpofe; often it confifteth in one knows not what, and fpringeth up one can hardly tell how. Its ways are unaccountable and inexplicable, being anfwerable to the numberlefs rovings of fancy and windings of language. It is, in fhort, a manner of fpeaking out of the fimple and plain way (fuch as reafon teacheth and proveth things by), which by a pretty furprifing uncouthnefs in conceit or expref-fion, doth affect and amufe the fancy, ftirring in it fome wonder, and breeding fome delight thereto."

It would not be difficult, and it would be an amufing paftime, to cull paffages from Shakefpere's plays which would anfwer to each of the various forms of wit here enumerated. *Falftaff* would fupply moft of them. That he who fo nimbly followed the turnings of this Proteus in his writings, was equally active in his converfation, Fuller, no mean judge, affures us; and we muft blame the reporters, or the nature of wit itfelf, if the jokes which have actually come down to us be difappoint-ing. I do not, however, feel at liberty to omit them.

From a collection of "Merry Paffages and Jefts,"

collected by Sir Nicholas l'Eftrange, we learn that on one occafion " Shakefpere was god-father to one of Ben Jonfon's children, and after the chriftening, being in a deep ftudy, Jonfon came to cheer him up, and afked him why he was fo melancholy. 'No, faith, Ben,' fays he, 'not I; but I have been confidering a great while what fhould be the fitteft gift for me to beftow upon my god-child, and I have refolved at laft.' 'I prithee what?' fays he. 'I' faith, Ben, I'll e'en give him a dozen latten (Latin) fpoons, and thou fhalt tranf-late them.' "

Now we muft recollect that Jonfon was a learned man, and probably was in the habit of poking fun at Shakefpere for his lack of Latin. Shakefpere retaliates by faying he will give the child fome latten, or brafs, fpoons, a ufual prefent from a fponfor, and that Jonfon fhall tranflate them, playing upon the am-biguity of the word *latten*, and hinting that Jonfon could do little but tranflate from the ancients. The joke is a good joke if we confider the circumftances, which, I think, muft have been pretty much what I have fuppofed. It is what Aulus Gellius calls a *fcomma*, and probably turned the laugh againft honeft Ben.

The next is not fo fuccefsful. We read in an Afh-molean MS. that " Mr. Ben Jonfon and Mr. William

Shakeſpere being merry at a tavern, Mr. Jonſon having begun this for his epitaph—

> ' Here lies Ben Jonſon,
> That was once one,'

he gives it to Mr. Shakeſpere to make up, who preſently writes—

> 'Who, while he lived, was a ſlow thing,
> And now, being dead, is no-thing.' "

No doubt Shakeſpere was a little out of patience with Jonſon's " ſlowneſs in his performance ; " his ending is certainly more pointed than Jonſon's beginning.

The two men ſeem to have been formed by nature, both from their reſemblance and the difference of their ſeveral charaćters, to be foils one to the other ; they went about together obſerving odd humours, and the faćt that they were always engaging in wit combats is one of the greateſt proofs of the ſincerity of their friendſhip. It is only a very ſincere affećtion that will bear the wear and tear of mutual jeſts, and none but men of a high order of intellećt and fine taſte can joke or take a joke without giving or taking offence.

Jonſon in his " Diſcoveries," in the ninth volume of Gifford's edition, ſays—" I remember the players have often mentioned it as an honour to Shakeſpere, that in his writing, whatſoever he penned he never blotted out a line. My anfwer hath been, 'Would he had blotted a thoufand!' which they thought a malevolent fpeech. I had not told pofterity this but for their ignorance, who chofe that circumftance to commend their friend by wherein he moft faulted, and to juftify mine own candour; for I loved the man and do honour his memory, on this fide idolatry, as much as any. He was, indeed, honeft, and of an open and free nature; had an excellent phantafy, brave notions, and gentle expreffions; wherein he flowed with that facility that fometimes it was neceffary he fhould be ftopped: *Sufflaminandus erat*, as Auguftus faid of Haterius. His wit was in his own power; would the rule of it had been fo too! Many times he fell into thofe things could not efcape laughter: as when he faid in the perfon of *Cæfar*, one fpeaking to him, 'Cæfar, thou doft me wrong,' he replied, 'Cæfar did never wrong but with juft caufe,' and fuch like, which were ridiculous. But he redeemed his vices with his virtues. There was ever more in him to be praifed than pardoned."

This is a piece of criticifm charaćteriftic of a correćt fcholar like Jonfon. That Shakefpere, writing with running pen, fhould have made fuch miftakes, was natural. It was as natural that Jonfon fhould be fcandalifed by them; but I, for one, am glad that Shake-

ſpere did not blot a line. We can well forgive ſuch an
Iriſh bull as Cæſar's reply, or ſuch a blunder as repreſenting a ſeaport in Bohemia—if it be a blunder, which
is doubtful, for I have ſeen it ſtated in ſome periodical
that ſeveral ſeaports on the Mediterranean formed part
of Bohemia in the ſixteenth century—in conſideration
of poſſeſſing the ſpontaneous flow of Shakeſpere's fine
genius. Sheridan uſed to ſay that your eaſy writing
was d——d hard reading, and this is generally true;
but Shakeſpere is really an entirely exceptional caſe.
Spontaneity is one of the peculiarities of his genius.
But it is abſurd to accuſe Jonſon—honeſt Ben—of
malignity for having his own view of his friend's
excellencies and defects. If we wanted a contradiction
to any ſuch accuſation it is to be found in his addreſs
to his departed friend. Jonſon's poems are ſo little
known to ordinary readers, and there is ſuch a charm
in his fine nervous Engliſh, that I make no excuſe
for giving the paſſage at length. How delightful is
ſtrength! There is no unpardonable ſin in art but
weakneſs, and for this there is no place of repentance.

> "To draw no envy, Shakeſpere, on thy name,
> Riſe I thus ample to thy book and fame;
> While I confeſs thy writings to be ſuch
> As neither man nor muſe can praiſe too much.
> 'Tis true, and all men's ſuffrage. But theſe ways
> Were not the paths I meant unto thy praiſe.

For fillieſt ignorance on theſe may light,
Which, when it founds at beſt, but echoes right;
Or blind affection, which doth ne'er advance
The truth, but gropes and urgeth all by chance;
Or crafty malice might pretend this praiſe,
And think to ruin where it ſeemed to raiſe.

  *   *   *   *   *   *   *

But thou art proof againſt them, and, indeed,
Above the ill-fortunè of them or their need.
I, therefore, will begin: Soul of the age!
The applauſe, delight, and wonder of the ſtage!
My Shakeſpere, riſe! I will not lodge thee by
Chaucer or Spenſer, or bid Beaumont lie
A little farther off to make thee room:
Thou art a monument without a tomb,
And art alive ſtill, while thy book doth live,
And we have wits to read, and praiſe to give.

  *   *   *   *   *   *   *

Yet muſt I not give Nature all: thy art,
My gentle Shakeſpere, muſt enjoy a part;
For though the poet's matter Nature be,
His art doth give the faſhion; and that he
Who caſts to write a living line muſt ſweat,
Such as thine are, and ſtrike the ſecond heat
Upon the Muſe's anvil; turn the ſame
And himſelf with it, that he thinks to frame;
Or for the laurel he may gain a ſcorn,
For a good poet 's made as well as born,
And ſuch wert thou! Look how the father's face
Lives in his iſſue; even ſo the race
Of Shakeſpere's mind and manners brightly ſhines
In his well-turnèd and true-filèd lines;
In each of which he ſeems to ſhake a lance,
As brandiſhed at the eyes of ignorance.
Sweet Swan of Avon! what a ſight it were
To ſee thee in our water yet appear,

> And make thofe flights upon the banks of Thames
> Which fo did take Eliza and our James!
> But ftay, I fee thee in the hemifphere
> Advanced, and made a conftellation there!
> Shine forth, thou ftar of poets! and with rage
> Or influence chide or cheer the drooping ftage,
> Which fince thy flight from hence hath mourned like night,
> And defpairs day, but for thy volume's light."

The other tribute to the memory of his friend was fubfcribed by Jonfon to Droefhout's engraving of Shakefpere, prefixed to the firft folio edition of his works publifhed in 1623, and attefts both Jonfon's affection and the fidelity of the likenefs :—

> " This figure that thou here feeft put,
> It was for gentle Shakefpere cut,
> Wherein the graver had a ftrife
> With Nature, to outdo the life.
> O, could he but have fhown his wit
> As well in brafs as he has hit
> His face, the print would then furpafs
> All that was ever writ in brafs!
> But fince he cannot, reader, look
> Not on his picture, but his book."

There is a paffage in Spenfer's "Teares of the Mufes" lamenting the death of "Willy." This has been referred to Shakefpere; but Mr. Dyce thinks it is inapplicable to Shakefpere, and that it was intended rather for Sir Philip Sidney, for Willy is a common name for all fhepherds, or, in paftoral language, poets; but there can be no doubt, from the allufion to the

name in the laſt lines of the following quotation from
" Colin Clout's come home again," that by Ætion is
meant Shakeſpere. Why he is called Ætion (Αιτιᾶν,
" one who aſks ") it is difficult to underſtand:—

> " And there, though laſt not leaſt, is Ætion ;
> A gentler ſhepherd may nowhere be found ;
> Whoſe Muſe, full of high thoughts' invention,
> Doth, like himſelf, heroically ſound."

Heaps of commendatory verſes from other meaner
poets might be quoted, but they would be rather dull
reading, and, after Ben Jonſon's fine and diſcriminating
lines, would ſeem very tame. The fact that Shakeſpere was commended and patroniſed by Elizabeth and
James implies, of courſe, that he was noticed and
careſſed by the courtiers.

Among such friends and companions was paſſed
Shakeſpere's town life ; but running parallel with it, as
it were, was another totally different life in the country. In London he was the favourite of princes
and great noblemen, the friend of the poets and men
of letters, and, as he laments in his ſonnet alrꞏ dy
quoted, dependent on the popular applauſe in a pro-
feſſion to which prejudice ſtill attached a note of
infamy. In his native Stratford we find him taking
his place among the gentry and ſubſtantial burgeſſes, a
farmer and a keen man of buſineſs, a man able to lend

a good round fum of money to a friend, one whofe influence was worth canvaffing for. His occupations in the country probably weaned him gradually from London, and about 1612 or 1613 he finally took up his abode at New Place with his family. Ward, the Vicar of Stratford, fays that "in his elder days he lived at Stratford, and fupplied the ftage with two plays every year, and for it had an allowance fo large that he fpent at the rate of one thoufand pounds a year," a fum equal to five times the amount at the prefent time.

From old deeds and records, hunted out with incredible zeal and labour by Shakefperian critics, and printed by Mr. Halliwell in his comprehenfive biography of the Poet, it appears that in 1612 he bought one hundred and feven acres of arable land at Stratford, of William Combe; alfo a cottage in Walker Street; in 1604 he brings an action againft Philip Rogers for £1 15*s*. 10*d*., owing to him for malt fupplied at different times; in 1605 he purchafes a moiety of the leafe of the tithes of Stratford and fome neighbouring parifhes; in 1612 he fues the other leffees of the tithes; in 1613 he defends his right to certain common lands; and all this time he is producing two plays a year.

In the meantime various changes take place in his family. In 1601 his father dies; in 1607 his eldeft daughter, Sufanna, marries Dr. Hall, a phyfician at

Stratford; in 1607 his firft grandchild, Elizabeth
Hall, is born, and in the fame year his mother, Mary
Arden, dies; in 1615 his fecond daughter, Judith,
whofe twin brother, Hamnet, had died fome confiderable time before, marries Thomas Quiney, vintner.

Rowe, his earlieft biographer, fays that his agreeable
manners and pleafant difpofition procured him the
friendfhip of the neighbouring gentry, and amongft the
reft, of a Mr. John Combe, who lived at the old
college from which the priefts had been expelled at the
Reformation. It feems to have been a favourite
amufement in thofe times for friends to write imaginary
epitaphs on each other over their wine. We have
feen already that Shakefpere and Ben Jonfon thus
diverted themfelves. A fimilar ftory is told of Charles
the Second and Buckingham, when the latter made
the celebrated epitaph on the " mutton-eating king."
Even Garrick, Reynolds, Burke, and Goldfmith played
at this fomewhat ghaftly game. A ftory then was
current that Mr. Combe, who was noted for his
ufurious practices, afked Shakefpere, when they were
making merry together, to write his epitaph, and that
Shakefpere produced the following :—

> "Ten in the hundred lies here engraved;
> 'Tis a hundred to ten his foul is not faved;
> If any man afks who lies in this tomb,
> Oh, oh! quoth the devil, 'tis my John-a-Combe."

Mr. Halliwell fays that this was a common joke in the jeft-books of the period, but perhaps Shakefpere thought it good enough for the occafion. Others hold that the ftory is difproved, becaufe the two men were friends, Combe leaving Shakefpere five pounds in his will, and Shakefpere in his bequeathing his fword to Combe's nephew, William. But, indeed, that friend-fhip muft be a frail commodity which could be broken by a joke like this. Mr. Combe was probably a faving man, and was certainly a rich one; and I have re-marked that rich and thrifty men are the laft people to be offended by a joke upon their clevernefs in amaffing money. As to prognofications on the company they are likely to keep in the next world, that is too unprac-tical a queftion to trouble them much. The joke was a poor one enough, and perhaps a ftale one too; but the ftory illuftrates the difficulty of catching that Proteus, wit, and binding him in the fetters of writing.

Another ftory, related to Malone by a native of Stratford, fays that Shakefpere being invited to a party by the topers of Bidford, a neighbouring village, made the following epigram on them and their neigh-bours :—

> "Piping Pebworth, dancing Marfton,
> Haunted Hillborough, and hungry Grafton,
> With dodging Exhall, papift Wixford,
> Beggarly Broom, and drunken Bidford."

Such tales as this are the only famples which tradition could feize upon to give pofterity an idea of the focial powers of the wittieft writer perhaps that ever exifted, and one whofe converfation is ftated by Fuller to have been remarkable for its verfatility and humour.

As I rode and walked about Stratford and the furrounding green lanes, and by the banks of the Avon, I could not help wondering whether the country people whom I met were aware that they were treading the ground which Shakefpere had trod while he was meditating " Cymbeline," " Coriolanus," the " Winter's Tale," and " The Tempeft." The thought of courfe was abfurd; the country people knew nothing about him, except that they fometimes got a fhilling from people who came to vifit his tomb; but my mind being wholly occupied with the memory of the mighty dead, it feemed to me as if they too muft be thinking of him. But very likely even his contemporaries, the burgeffes and country gentlemen with whom he affociated, admitted him to their fociety, not becaufe he was a great poet, but becaufe he was a wealthy man and a pleafant companion, who could tell them ftories of the great world in London. His plays were not publifhed collectively till feven years after his death, and very likely few of the feparate editions made their way down to Stratford. The burgeffes, Shakefpere's fellow-citizens, had actually forbidden the reprefentation of ftage plays in the town, and we may, therefore, conclude that they would regard the arch-playwright as "little better than one of the wicked." Sir Walter Scott complained that fome vifitors at Abbotsford were too poetical for him; and I fancy that Shakefpere would have had the fame fort of feeling with regard to his art, and that any unobfervant perfon feeing him at home would have fcarcely believed that he was the author of the plays. There would have been very little of what we fhould call "the fhop" about him.

His farms, his malting afforded him active occupation; but for exercifing his great intellectual powers in works which kept his name alive amongft the great ones of the earth, he found time; and it is not a little remarkable that fome of the fineft of his plays were written after his retirement to the country, as if his genius were there moft free and vigorous. His amufements were probably thofe fo quaintly defcribed by his contemporary, Burton :—"The ordinary fports which are ufed abroad [out of doors] are hawking, hunting : *hilares venandi labores*, one calls them, becaufe they recreate body and mind; another *the beft exercife that is, by which alone many have been freed from all feral difeafes.* Hegefippus (lib. i., cap. 37) relates of

Herod that he was eafed of a grievous melancholy by
that means. Plato (7 *de leg.*) highly magnifies it,
dividing it into three parts—by land, water, air.
Xenophon (in *Cyropæd.*) graces it with a great name,
Deorum munus, the gift of the gods, a princely fport,
which they have ever ufed, faith Langius (Epift. 59,
lib. ii.), fole almoft and ordinary fport of our noblemen
in Europe, and elfewhere all over the world. Bohemus
(*De Mor. Gent.,* lib. iii., cap. 12) ftiles it therefore
ftudium nobilium; 'tis all their ftudy, their exercife,
ordinary bufinefs, all their talk; and indeed fome
dote too much after it; they can do nothing elfe,
difcourfe of naught elfe. Paulus Jovius (*Defcr. Brit.*)
doth in fome fort tax our Englifh nobility for it, for
living in the country fo much, and too frequent ufe of
it, as if they had no other means but hawking and
hunting to approve themfelves gentlemen with.

" Hawking comes near to hunting, the one in the
air as the other on the earth, a fport as much affected
as the other, by fome preferred. It was never heard of
amongft the Romans, invented fome 1,200 years fince,
and firft mentioned by Firmicus (lib. v., cap. 8). The
Greek emperors began it, and now nothing fo frequent;
he is nobody that in the feafon hath not a hawk on his
fift : a great art, and many books written on it. * * *
The Mufcovian emperors reclaim eagles to fly at hinds,

foxes, &c., and fuch a one was fent for a prefent to Queen Elizabeth: fome reclaim ravens, caftrels, pies, &c., and train them for their pleafures.

" Fowling is more troublefome, but all out as delight-fome to fome forts of men, be it with guns, lime, nets, glades, ginnes, ftrings, baits, pitfalls, pipes, calls, ftalking-horfes, fetting-dogs, coy-ducks, or otherwife. Some much delight to take larks with day nets, fmall birds with draff-nets, plovers, partrich, herons, fnite, &c. * * * Tycho Brahe, that great aftronomer, in the chorography of his Ifle of Huena and Caftle of Uraneburge, puts down his nets and manner of catching fmall birds as an ornament and a recreation, wherein he himfelf was fometimes employed." * * *

After enumerating fifhing, which he terms " a kind of hunting by water," ringing, bowling, fhooting, " keelpins, tronks, coits, pitching bars, hurling, wreftling, leaping, running, fencing, muftring, fwim-ming, wafters, foils, foot-balls, balowns, quintans, &c., and many fuch, which are the common recreations of the country folks; riding of great horfes, running at rings, tilts and turnaments, horfe races, wild-goofe chafes, which are the difports of greater men, and good in themfelves, though many gentlemen by that means gallop quite out of their fortunes;" he comes to " *deam-bulatio per amœna loca,* to make a petty progrefs, a

merry journey now and then with some good company, to visit a friend, see cities, castles, towns,

' Visere sæpe amnes nitidos, peramœnaque Tempe,
    Et placidas summis sectari in montibus auras'

    (To see the pleasant fields, the cryftal fountains,
    And take the gentle air among the mountains);

to walk amongst orchards, gardens, bowers, mounts,
and arbours, artificial wildernesses, green thickets,
arches, groves, lawns, and such like pleasant places,
like that Antiochian Daphne, brooks, pools, fish-ponds,
betwixt wood and water, in a fair meadow, by a river
side, *ubi variæ avium cantationes, florum colores, pra-
torum frutices, &c.*, to disport in some pleasant plain,
park, run up a steep hill sometimes, or sit in a shady
seat, must needs be a delectable recreation."

His enumeration of games for winter evenings is still
fuller and more various. "The ordinary recreations
which we have in winter, and in most solitary times
busy our minds with, are cards, tables, and dice,
shovel-board, chess play, the philosopher's game, small
trunks, shuttle-cock, billiards, music, masks, singing,
dancing, ulegames, frolicks, jests, riddles, catches,
purposes, questions and commands, merry tales of
errant knights, queens, lovers, lords, ladies, giants,
dwarfs, thieves, cheaters, witches, fairies, goblins, friars,
&c., such as the old women told Psyche in Apuleius,

Boccace novels, and the rest, *quorum auditione pueri delectantur, senes narratione*, which some delight to hear, some to tell."

Such were probably the amusements and employments in which Shakespere passed his latter days; for he, no doubt, lived and amused himself like his neighbours in Stratford and its vicinity. He did not quit the Court and the society of London that he might spend his time in poring over books in the country.

But, as Cowley, another poet, who fought for quiet in rural retirement, and healthful employment in the cultivation of a farm, complains:—" God laughs at man who says to his soul, *Take thy ease :* I met presently not only with many little incumbrances and impediments, but with so much sickness (a new misfortune to me) as would have spoiled the happiness of an emperor as well as mine : yet I do neither repent nor alter my course. *Non ego perfidum Dixi sacramentum ;* nothing shall separate me from a mistress [retirement] which I have loved so long and have now at last married, though she neither has brought me a rich portion, nor lived yet so quietly with me as I hoped from her.

'Nec vos dulcissima mundi
Nomina, vos Musæ, libertas, otia, libri,
Hortique, sylvæque animâ remanente relinquam.'

(Nor by me e'er fhall you,
You of all names the fweeteft and the beft,
You, mufes, books, and liberty, and reft,
You, gardens, fields, and woods, forfaken be,
As long as life itfelf forfakes not me.)"

And fo difeafe and death overtook Shakefpere as they did Cowley, in that retreat where they both had hoped to find the reft which fate had hitherto denied them.

New Place had probably been a fcene of much feftivity on February 10, 1615. Judith, Shakefpere's younger daughter, had been married to Thomas Quiney, his fellow townfman, and no doubt there was a gathering of all the family, and the wedding party walked up to the beautiful church, and paffed in through the porch and under the folar, of which Mr. Erneft Edwards has given us fuch a charming little picture, and there was a banquet, and the "brod filver and gilt bole" was filled with "canaris fack," and there was a dance, and probably a play or interlude was acted in the hall. And this was, perhaps, the occafion of Jonfon's and Drayton's vifit to their old friend, when, according to Ward, these three "had a merrie meeting, and it feems drank too hard, for Shakefpere died of a fever there contracted." Whatever may have been the caufe of his death, it is certain that he died on the 23rd of April, 1616, a little more than two

months after his daughter's marriage, and that the
fignatures in his will fhow that his hand was unfteady
when he figned it. It was executed on the 5th of
March, 1616.

Whether Ward's teftimony be worth much, feeing
that it dates fifty years at leaft after the event, is a
queftion. Indeed it seems to have been thought the
correct thing to reprefent a poet, and efpecially a
dramatic poet, to have died of hard living, as Anacreon
is faid to have been choked by a grape-ftone. Puritanifm, which was then coming into vogue, and which
always fuppofes itfelf to be in the fecrets of Providence,
thought perhaps to fhow by this means that Heaven
was bound to punifh, not only in the next world, but
even in this, the heinous fin of having written good
poetry. Shakefpere was profperous; their theory therefore would not hold if it appeared that he who had
held up the godly to ridicule by reprefenting a Puritan
as " finging pfalms to hornpipes " had died like other
men. Shakefpere very likely rejoiced to fhow his
country hofpitality and warm houfekeeping to Jonfon
and Drayton, his countryman, and he may have
fickened with fever foon after. It was eafy to fay *poft
hoc, ergo, propter hoc*, though it was probably not hock
but fherry that they drank. And that there were
plenty of perfons at Stratford who would be glad to tell

Ward, the vicar, a ftory to the difadvantage of the wild youth who had broken Sir Thomas Lucy's park, and afterwards become richer than they by writing and acting plays, human nature and the nature of Puritanifm forbid us to doubt. With Puritans Stratford muft have abounded, inafmuch as we find that ftage-plays, as was before obferved, had been forbidden there by the municipal authorities. We need not, therefore, believe that gentle Shakefpere met his death in this untoward fafhion. The tradition may have originated in a pious defire to blacken the name of a writer of plays.

Perhaps to the fame caufe may be traced the report of Davies, that " he dyed a Papift." His father was included in a lift of perfons who abfented themfelves from the reformed fervice at church, and of whom cognizance was taken for that offence by the penal laws of the time; but it is ftated that the reafon was not recufancy, but the fear of arreft. I am not aware of the date of the law which allows the debtor immunity from arreft on Sunday, but an eminent lawyer has informed me that it is part of that common law which derives its authority from the fact of its having been a cuftom " whereof the memory of man runneth not to the contrary," that is to fay, traceable to the reign of Richard the Second. The allegation may, therefore, have been an excufe. The teftimony of Davies and of the corporation archives at Stratford is, however, confirmed in fome degree by a document faid to have been difcovered in the houfe in Henley Street in 1770. Thomas Hart, a defcendant of John Shakefpere, employed a mafon named Mofeley to repair the roof of one of the houfes there. Mofeley alleged that in the courfe of his work he found a manufcript hidden beneath the tiling, and this manufcript purported to be written by John Shakefpere, and to be a profeffion of his faith as a Roman Catholic. It has been publifhed, and is indeed thoroughly anti-proteftant. It was accepted at firft as genuine by Malone, but he afterwards rejeéted it. Chalmers maintains its genuinenefs. Againft this it is argued that John Shakefpere muft have taken the oath of allegiance on becoming a bailiff and alderman; but on the other hand he was depofed from thefe offices; and it by no means follows that becaufe he once conformed, he may not afterwards have changed his mind. It is an hiftorical faét that a great many perfons who, in the beginning of the queen's reign, attended the reformed worfhip, withdrew themfelves when the bull of Pope Pius V., iffued in 1563, drew an impaffable line of demarcation between Roman Catholics and Anglicans.

But it by no means follows that becaufe John Shakefpere was a recufant, his fon was one too. There are fome paffages in the plays which fhow no good-will to the caufe of the Pope; as in " King John "—

> " *King John.* What earthly name to interrogatories
> Can talk the free breath of a facred king?
> Thou canft not, cardinal, devife a name
> So flight, unworthy, and ridiculous,
> To charge me to an anfwer, as the pope.
> Tell him this tale; and from the mouth of England,
> Add this much more,—that no Italian prieft
> Shall tithe or toll in our dominions;
> But as we under heaven are fupreme head,
> So, under him, that great fupremacy,
> Where we do reign, we will alone uphold
> Without the affiftance of a mortal hand.
> So tell the pope; all reverence fet apart,
> To him, and his ufurped authority."

But, on the other hand, there is nothing anti-papal in " Henry the Eighth," where we might have expected to find it; and even in the paffage above quoted the proteft of King John is political, not doctrinal, and fuch as a Gallican might have ufed in the reign of Louis the Fourteenth.

It would be endlefs to quote paffages to fhow how deeply imbued Shakefpere was with the old theology. In "Hamlet" the ghoft of the king declares that he has been releafed for a term from purgatory, and complains that he did not receive the Viaticum and the facrament of Extreme Unction :—

" Thus was I, fleeping, by a brother's hand
  Of life, of crown, of queen, at once defpatch'd :
  Cut off even in the bloffoms of my fin,
  Unhoufel'd, difappointed. unanel'd.'

I think, too, we may trace an allufion to the religious
changes, backwards and forwards, which diftracted the
nation in the reigns of Henry the Eighth, Edward the
Sixth, Mary and Elizabeth, in the faying in " Lear,"
" It is and it is not, is no good divinity ; " or perhaps
the paffage may allude to the ambiguity of the Angli-
can formularies, which were framed to include both
Catholics and Proteftants. But certainly monks and
friars are generally treated with refpect in the plays,
while the parochial clergy, who were generally
favourers of the new doctrine, are held up to ridicule
in fuch characters as *Sir Hugh Evans* and *Sir Nathaniel.*

A very curious entry in the Chamberlain's accounts
at Stratford under the year 1614, is ftill extant :—
" Item, for on quart of fack, and on quart of clarett
winne, given to a preacher at the New Place, XXd."
Now, whether this preacher were fent to try and
convert Shakefpere, or whether he came by the Poet's
wifh is uncertain ; but if the latter, the corporation
would not have paid for his reverence's liberal pota-
tions. Indeed it was quite in the fpirit of the age to
fend a preacher to a man's houfe for the exprefs purpofe of refuting his religious belief.

From his writings I fhould rather imagine that Shakefpere, as far as religion was concerned, refembled the great ftatefmen of Henry and Elizabeth—politically they were Proteftants, doctrinally Catholics, and were willing to fubmit outwardly to the powers in being, while they held themfelves free to have their own private opinions, which were not thofe of the vulgar, and far from fanatical.

The Poet's illnefs muft have lafted a confiderable time, for his will is dated the 5th of March, and the fignatures to it, by their tremulous lines, fhow that he muft have been very weak when he wrote them. The houfe of rejoicing had foon been turned into the houfe of mourning; in February New Place rang with the merriment of a bridal; in April the mafter lay dead in one of its chambers. Shakefpere's laft teftament fhows the fame kindly difpofition as was difplayed in his whole life. After, in the ufual form, commending his foul to God, he leaves the bulk of his perfonal property to his elder daughter, Mrs. Hall; and to his fecond daughter, Mrs. Quiney, and his nephews and nieces, fons of Mrs. Joan Hart, his fifter, certain fums of money; to Mrs. Hall all his plate, except his " brod filver-gilt bole ;" to the poor of the parifh ten pounds; to Mr. Thomas Combe his fword; to Thomas Ruffell and Francis Collins fmall fums; and to Hamlet Sadleir, William Raynolds, William Walker, his godfon, Anthonye Nafhe, and to "my fellows, John Hemynges, Richard Burbage, and Henry Cundell," fmall fums of money "to buy themfelves rings." His fecond beft bed he leaves to his wife; but at any rate, as has been already obferved, fhe had her dower and thirds at common law out of all his freehold property, and was therefore amply provided for. The moft noticeable point, however, is his kind remembrances of his fellow actors and partners in the theatre.

In the next century Shakefpere's family became extinct. His daughter Sufanna, married to John Hall, died in 1649, leaving one daughter, married firft to Thomas Nafh, and fecondly to John (afterwards Sir John) Barnard of Abington in Northamptonfhire, but fhe died without iffue, and was buried at Abington in 1669.

Judith, married to Thomas Quiney, had three children: Shakefpere, baptifed November 23, 1616, and buried May 8, 1617; Richard, baptifed February 9, 1617-18, and buried February 26, 1638-9; and Thomas, baptifed January 23, 1619-20, and buried January 28, 1638-9. She herfelf was buried in Stratford Church on February 9, 1661-2.

A Mrs. Hornby, a defcendant of the Poet's fifter,

Joan Hart, was living till lately at Stratford, and ufed to gain her livelihood by fhowing the houfe in Henley Street to ftrangers. She was quite illiterate, and was much vexed when the houfe was purchafed to be reftored.

. Like Milton and Sir Walter Scott, Shakefpere has left no lineal defcendant to inherit his name or his genius.

By the Poet's untimely death, when he was only fifty-two, and therefore ftill in the zenith of his powers, pofterity loft the chance of obtaining a full and correct collection of his works. Whether he ever would have collected and edited them is, however, doubtful. Even his fonnets, which were publifhed in his lifetime, appear to have been given to the public without his con-currence. He feems, indeed, to have been like the oftrich in the Pfalms, which the Lord is faid to have deprived of underftanding, fo that fhe leaves her eggs in the fand to be hatched by the heat of the fun, or to be trodden down by the foot of the wayfarer, as chance may order it. Yet for the fake of the money at leaft, which might have purchafed another farm or two at Stratford, it may be fuppofed that he would have entered into a fpeculation which might have proved profitable. Then we fhould have had no emendators; no Bentleys, no Irelands, no Colliers, and one great branch of literary induftry would never have exifted.

Neverthelefs, the certainty that we were reading what Shakefpere really did mean to fay might have confoled us even for this lofs.

The taſk of collecting his plays, was referved for his " fellows," John Heminge and Henry Condell, whom he had named in his will; and under their fuperintendence was publifhed, feven years after his death, the firſt folio edition of his dramatic works. It is dedicated to William, Earl of Pembroke, the Lord Chamberlain, and to Philip, Earl of Montgomery.

The addrefs, " To the great variety of readers," prefixed to this edition is interefting :—

" From the moſt able to him that can but fpell: there you are numbered. We had rather you were weighed : efpecially when the fate of all books depends upon your capacities ; and not of your heads alone but of your purfes. Well, it is now public, and you will ſtand for your privileges we know,—to read and cenfure. Do fo, but buy it firſt ; that doth beſt commend a book, the ſtationer fays. Then how odd foever your brains be or your wifdoms, make your licenfe the fame and fpare not. Judge your fix penn'orth, your ſhilling's worth, or your five ſhillings' worth at a time, or higher, fo you rife to the proof rates, and welcome. But, whatever you do, buy. Cenfure will not drive a trade or make the Jack go. And though you be a magiſtrate of wit, and fit on the ſtage at Blackfriars or the Cock-pit, to arraign plays daily, know thefe plays have had their trial already, and ſtood out all appeals, and do now come forth quitted rather by a decree of court than any purchafed letters of commendation.

" It had been a thing, we confefs, worthy to be wiſhed, that the author himfelf had lived to have fet forth and overfeen his own writings. But

fince it hath been ordained otherwife, and he by death departed from
that right, we pray you do not envy his friends the office of their care
and pain, to have collected and publifhed them ; and fo to have publifhed
them, as where (before) you were abufed with divers ftolen and furrep-
titious copies, maimed and deformed by the frauds and ftealths of injurious
impoftors, that expofed them, even thofe are now offered to your view
cured and perfect of their limbs, and all the reft abfolute in their numbers
as he conceived them; who, as he was a happy imitator of nature, was a
moft gentle expreffer of it : his mind and hands went together ; and
what he thought he uttered with that eafinefs that we have fcarce
received from him a blot on his paper. But it is not our province, who
only gather his works and give them you, to praife him. It is yours that
read him ; and then we hope, to your divers capacities, you will find
enough both to draw and hold you, for his wit can no more lie hid than
it can be loft. Read him therefore ; and again and again ; and if then
you do not like him, furely you hunger not to underftand him. And fo
we leave you to other of his friends, whom, if you need, can be your
guides : if you need them not, you can lead yourfelves and others. And
fuch readers we wifh him.

"JOHN HEMINGE.
"HENRY CONDELL."

It is needlefs perhaps to fay that in this edition the
plays are very far indeed from being "cured and perfect
of their limbs, and all the reft abfolute of their
numbers." If fo we fhould not have our attention
drawn off from fome neceffary action of the play
by having to look at a note to explain an unintelligible paffage. But this firft folio, as it is called,
has been generally taken as the foundation of fubfequent texts, and has been adopted as fuch by the
editors of the fcholarlike Cambridge edition, now in
courfe of publication.

CHAPTER XI.

IT now remains to notice the few memorials of the Poet which are preferved in different places throughout the town. Firft there is Mr. James's mufeum of Shakefperian relics, confifting of various pieces of furniture faid to have been taken from New Place. Then there is the Town Hall, where may be feen a picture of the Poet by Wilfon, idealifed from the buft; but I confefs the original is more interefting to me. How could Wilfon tell that Shakefpere looked more poetical than the buft reprefents him to have looked? Then there is an affected picture of Garrick leaning on Shakefpere's buft, and looking as if he actually believed the nonfenfe which people talked, about his rivalling the genius of the Poet himfelf. Fancy Davy patron-ifing Shakefpere, and thinking that he knew better than the author of "The Tempeft" what was fuited to the ftage! Though Burke and the other members of the club combined to flatter him, fturdy old Samuel Johnfon was much nearer a true eftimation of his merits. The

very fact that he prefumed to alter and adapt Shakefpere's plays, is, to my mind, proof pofitive that, whatever his powers of declamation, he muft have been a
very little man indeed. Romney's portrait of the Duke
of Dorfet is alfo to be feen here, and is well worth looking at. On a fcreen may be obferved ridiculous pictures
of the mummery which was acted in the ftreets of
Stratford under Garrick's aufpices at the Jubilee in the
laft century. It is devoutly to be hoped that the Poet's
memory may not be defecrated by a repetition of fuch
folly next Spring. The worft of it is, that on all fuch
occafions that refpectable body called, in the language
of the gods, "licenfed victuallers," and in that of men,
"publicans," has generally as influential a voice as it
has in the election of members for Marylebone and
the Tower Hamlets. Any vulgar fhow, therefore,
which will fill the public-houfes, will be fure to have
many advocates at Stratford.

But the moft interefting relic of all, which, as it
comes laft in the order of the Poet's life, I kept for the
laft ftation of my pilgrimage, is the church where his
bones repofe. It is, in itfelf, a noble ftructure, furrounded by fine trees, and built on the bank of the
beautiful Avon, which on one fide bounds the church-
yard. As I approached it under an avenue of lime
trees I thought how often the Poet had trodden the

same path. Here he had probably learned his first
lessons in divinity, upon which his works show that he
had thought deeply and accurately. Hither he had
accompanied the christening party, when his children,
Susanna, Hamnet, and Judith had been baptised.
Here he had joined the crowd of his fellow-citizens in
after days when they were "knolled to parish church,"
and endured the prosing of some worthy preacher, who
endeavoured to soothe the fidgettiness of his congregation
with, "Have patience, good people; have patience;"
or sat amused upon his bench while "coughing
drowned the parson's saw." Here he followed the
bier of his only son with sorrow to the grave, and
hither he himself was borne at last, when all too soon
he left the world of which he was the benefactor, and
will be till the crack of doom; for divines may preach
and philosophers may theorise, but what philosopher
or divine will ever convey such lessons of practical
wisdom, or speak so inwardly to the conscience as the
writer of "Hamlet," "Lear," and "Othello?"

But I was recalled from these thoughts by a woman
with a broom in her hand, who, like the vulture of the
desert, seemed to nose from afar the prey which had
come within her reach. However, I felt a sort of dis-
inclination to enter too suddenly upon the *intima
penetralia* of the temple, and made my approaches

with deliberation; juft as one fometimes anxioufly fcans
the poftmark on the outfide of a letter and the hand-
writing of the direction, when by fimply breaking the
feal all myftery might at once be diffipated.

I therefore began by walking round the church, and
found that it was built of grey ftone, in the form of a
crofs, with large chancel and tower at its junction with
the nave; tranfepts, aifles, and north porch. There
are fome Romanefque remains and early Englifh work in
the ftructure; but the chief part is perpendicular, of the
fourteenth century. The guide-book informed me
that the fouth aifle was rebuilt by John de Stratford,
Archbifhop of Canterbury, in the reign of Edward the
Third. The chancel appears to be the lateft part of
the building, and was probably rebuilt or largely altered
in the fifteenth century. The college for priefts,
where John-a-Combe once refided, and which muft
have been one of the greateft ornaments of the town,
was actually pulled down in 1799 by its then owner, a
Mr. Edward Butterfbee.

On entering by the beautiful porch, furmounted by
its folar, where a prieft probably once kept fchool, the
view is very impofing; you can fee from the weft to
the eaft window, and can appreciate fully the extraordinary inclination of the chancel towards the fouth,
for there are no high pews to intercept the vifion.

The church has been, what is called, "reftored," and
the people fit on low benches. This procefs has not
been done in the beft of tafte indeed, and the aifles are
ftill encumbered with galleries; but I do not think the
ftructure of the church itfelf has been materially injured. As I advanced up towards the eaft end, I
obferved a chapel in the north aifle filled with fine
monuments of the Clopton family, amongft which the
alabafter figures of George Carew, Earl of Totnefs and
Baron Clopton, with his countefs, coloured to refemble
life, are the moft curious.

And now I approached the very fpot in which re-
pofes all that was mortal of Shakefpere. The chancel
is, on the whole, a worthy fhrine for fuch a relic. The
old *mifereres* or feats for the choir remain, and are
curious examples of the grotefque tafte of the latter
part of the middle ages; for each feat, on being turned
up, difclofes fome quaint and hideous figures, which
are not certainly conducive to religious ideas, nor
indeed quite decent. But of courfe, the object of all
objects is the grave itfelf of Shakefpere. It is beneath
the dais on which ftands the altar, and is covered by a
flag-ftone, which bears the infcription—

> "Good frend, for Jefvs fake forbeare
> To digg the dvft encloofed heare;
> Blefte be ye man yt fpares thes ftones,
> And cvrft be he yt moves my bones."

This piece of foolish doggrel, which is common enough on tomb-ftones, has been, I believe, by fome, fuppofed to have been written by the Poet himfelf. I cannot believe that he could have been fo fuperftitious and egotiftical—he who cared fo little what became of the creations of his mind would furely be ftill lefs folicitous about the duft which formed his body. He who had fo meditated on life and death as to write the fcene at *Ophelia's* grave, could not have cared much what became of his bones :—

"*Hamlet.* To what bafe ufes may we return, Horatio! Why may not imagination trace the noble duft of Alexander till he find it ftopping a bung-hole?

Horatio. 'Twere to confider too curioufly to confider fo.

Hamlet. No, faith, not a jot ; but to follow him thither with modefty enough, and likelihood to lead it : as thus; Alexander died; Alexander was buried; Alexander returned unto duft; the duft is earth; of earth we make loam; and why of that loam, whereto he was converted, might they not ftop a beer-barrel?"

It is not to be fuppofed that Shakefpere could vehemently defire for his remains an immunity from the chances which might befall thofe of Alexander.

Within a few yards of the grave, againft the north wall of the chancel, is the celebrated monument. Mr. Edwards gives the reader a photographic fac-fimile of it. It is in itfelf not in bad tafte, except for the naked little boys at the top, and the effigy is probably the beft likenefs of the Poet extant. Digges,

in his verſes prefixed to the firſt folio edition of the
plays, publiſhed in 1623, mentions it, and therefore it
muſt have been erected ſoon after the poet's death.
The tradition is that it was done by Gerard Johnſon
from a caſt taken after death; and curiouſly enough
ſuch a caſt was lately in the poſſeſſion of a German
phyſician, and is now, I believe, in Profeſſor Owen's
hands. It was originally coloured to repreſent life, for
the artiſts of thoſe days had no idea but to "hold the
mirror up to nature;" nor did they ſee any propriety
in repreſenting the human form of a dead white colour.
Shakeſpere, ſpeaking of the ſuppoſed ſtatue of *Hermione*, calls it "a piece many years in doing, and now
newly performed by that rare Italian maſter, Julio
Romano." Now this muſt have been ſuppoſed to have
been painted to reſemble life, becauſe when *Perdita* is
about to kiſs its hand, *Paulina* ſays.

> " O, patience !
> The ſtatue is but newly fixed, the colours
> Not dry."

And again, when *Leontes* is going to kiſs the lips
Paulina interrupts him :—

> " Good, my lord, forbear ;
> The ruddineſs upon her lip is wet ;
> You'll mar it if you kiſs it ; ſtain your own
> With oily painting."

It ſhewed, therefore, great ignorance in Malone to

have the buft painted ftone colour, as if that were more
claffical, when in reality we know that the Greeks and
Romans painted the pureft Parian marble; but Malone,
in this, was only following the falfe tafte of his age,
and therefore I think he is rather harfhly treated in
the following epigram, infcribed by a vifitor in the
book appropriated to fignatures and obfervations:—

> " Stranger, to whom this monument is fhown,
> Invoke the Poet's curfe upon Malone;
> Whofe meddling zeal his barbarous tafte betrays,
> And daubs his tombftone as he mars his plays."

Malone's annotations and fuggeftions certainly did not
mar the poet's plays, though it is true that the ftone-
coloured paint betrayed a barbarous tafte in art.

A few years ago the ftone-coloured paint was removed, and the old colours renewed. The hair, mouf-
tachios, and beard are now reprefented as chefnut, the
eyes, I think, brown, and the complexion ruddy. The
Poet is reprefented dreffed in "his habit as he lived."
It will be feen that he appears in the act of compofition,
and from the expreffion of his face it is to be prefumed
that the work upon which he is engaged is a comedy;
there is indeed a certain fmirk upon the features, but
this is owing in great meafure to the curl of the mouf-
tachios and the fhadow they caft upon the mouth.
But the whole face expreffes high intelligence and

genial good humour, and in this is much fuperior to the other portraits of him, and efpecially to the Chandos, and the engraving in the folio edition of his works, publifhed in 1623.

On the flab beneath the buft is the following infcription, which I will give for the benefit of my more elderly readers; the younger, with the help of a magnifying glafs, may decipher it themfelves, from Mr. Edwards's photograph :—

JUDICIO PYLIVM, GENIO SOCRATEM, ARTE MARONEM
TERRA TEGIT, POPVLVS MŒRET, OLYMPVS HABET.

" STAY, PASSENGER, WHY GOEST THOV BY SO FAST,
READ, IF THOV CANST, WHOM ENVIOVS DEATH HATH PLAST
WITHIN THIS MONVMENT, SHAKESPERE, WITH WHOME
QVICK NATVRE DIDE ; WHOSE NAME DOTH DECK Yᵉ TOMBE
FAR MORE THAN COST, SITH ALL Yᵗ HE HATH WRITT
LEAVES LIVING ART BVT PAGE TO SERVE HIS WITT."
" Obiit Ano Doi 1616, Ætatis 53, die 23 Ap."

Befide Shakefpere's grave, to the fouth, is that of Anne Hathaway, his wife (see ante, p. 57). On the fouth fide lies Mrs. Sufanna Hall, his eldeft daughter, who died in 1649. On her tombftone the original verfes have been renewed, for they had been obliterated, and run as follows :—

" Witty above her fexe, but that 's not all,
Wise to falvation was good Miftrefs Hall :
Something of Shakefpere was in that, but this
Wholly of Him of whom fhe's now in bliffe.

> Then paffenger, haft ne'ere a teare
>   To weep with her that wept with all ?
> That wept, yet fet herfelf to chere
>   Them up with comfort's cordiall.
> Her love fhall live, her mercy fpread,
> When thou haft ne'er a tear to fhed."

Some have thought that the fourth line is a reflection upon her father, as if fhe inherited none of her good difpofitions from him; but in reality it only fhows that the writer not only liked to make an epigrammatic antithefis, but was an orthodox anti-pelagian, and held the utter corruption of human nature. On the fame line, below the altar, are the tombs of Mrs. Judith Quiney, Shakefpere's younger daughter, and Elizabeth, his grand-daughter, married firft to Thomas Nafh, and afterwards to Sir John Barnard, and befide them, that of Dr. Hall. To the north of the altar, againft the eaft wall, is a handfome tomb erected to the memory of John-a-Combe, the Poet's friend.

Thofe who defire to fee the very entries themfelves of the births, deaths, and marriages in the Shakefpere family, will find them in the regifter. Malone has printed them in his edition of the Poet's works.

All that now remains to be noticed is the broken font in the veftry, in which Shakefpere himfelf and his children were probably baptifed. It is placed on the

parish cheſt, and has been photographed by Mr. Erneſt Edwards.

The old buildings and other remains of the England of Shakeſpere's day are faſt paſſing away. The true " Herne's Oak," was felled, I believe, in the laſt century, and a very old tree in Windſor Park, which local tradition had ſubſtituted for it, was blown down ſhortly before I undertook my pilgrimage. The "Boar's Head " in Eaſtcheap has long ſince diſappeared with its " fly-bitten tapeſtries," and the inn at Rocheſter, of which the carrier declared that " this be the moſt villainous houſe in all London Road for fleas," has juſt been pulled down to make way for a railroad. Of the ſtatue which graces " Poets' Corner " in Weſt-minſter Abbey, and was erected in the laſt century, Mr. Edwards gives us a photograph. The attitude and drapery are graceful, but neither the face nor figure bear the ſmalleſt reſemblance to thoſe of the Poet as he is ſeen in the Stratford monument, from which we learn that his outward as well as his inward man repreſented the honeſt, manly, unſentimental Engliſh-man—the typical John Bull.

Next day, being Sunday, I joined the groups who hurried along the, till then, deſerted ſtreets of Stratford to morning prayers, and found that the ſervice was conducted in a manner worthy of the fine church

and its great affociations. Almoft the whole was
fung by a well-trained choir, and very fine and im-
preffive it was. But when the clergyman mounted the
pulpit to preach, I foon found that the fermon was
fadly out of tune with the time, the place, and the reft
of the proceedings. It was, in fact, a fcolding to the
parifhioners for not coming to the Sacrament. Now I
hate all fcolding, and do not believe in it ; and, moreover, this particular fcolding did not apply to me ; while
it lafted, therefore, I had leifure to let my mind roam
over the paft and revel in the affociations of the place.
And when the final bleffing was given I could hardly
prevail on myfelf to leave the laft fcene—the conclud-
ing ftation of my pilgrimage.

   With my vifit to the church on Sunday, and long
lingering look at the marble beneath which repofe the
bones of Shakefpere, my pilgrimage to Stratford came
to an end. Thinking that I fhould fpend the Sunday
afternoon quite as well in riding along the pretty roads
of Warwickfhire as in falling afleep in my inn over
fuch volume of old fermons as I might borrow from
my landlady, I mounted little Stornoway, and, accompanied by Smoker, turned my face towards home.
On my road the horfe-boys feemed much furprifed to
fee me returning fo foon, for they had foretold that I
fhould never reach my deftination ; but they did not

know Stornoway's capabilities. I, who do know them, am happy to fay that he has now taken up his permanent abode in my ftable. Some few weeks after my return I happened to pay the friend who had lent him to me a vifit, and as we walked through the fields attached to the houfe, Stornoway came trotting up and thruft his pretty nofe into the breaft of my coat, thus fhowing his remembrance of my care of him during our joint pilgrimage. The refult was, that he tranf-ferred his allegiance to me next morning, and now carries me about to vifit in my parifh, where he is the admiration and pet of everybody.

Smoker's travels have not, I think, improved him. He has grown too much a citizen of the world. His frequent vifits to inns have given him a tafte for fuch haunts; and now, when I take him to Chelmsford, he makes himfelf fo comfortable among the horfes and horfe-boys, that he fcarcely cares to return home. But his friendfhip for Stornoway is unabated, and they occupy the fame bed at night.

I myfelf am more than ever convinced of the benefit conferred on mind and body by fuch a trip as I have defcribed; but the next time I ride abroad, it fhall be with a companion, efpecially if England be the fcene of my pilgrimage.

CHAPTER XII.

My experiment has now been made, and as far as I am concerned, it has proved fuccefsful. My pilgrimage to Shakefpere's birth-place, home, and grave, combined with the few facts and traditions refpecting him which have come down to us, and with the fplendid legacy which in his works he has bequeathed to mankind, have enabled me to form a certain ideal of the man. Whether that ideal be true or fantaftical; whether it will recommend itfelf to others or not, I cannot tell; but, at any rate, I am fatisfied with it.

In the firft place, then, Shakefpere was a manly man, fond of the fports which make Englifhmen quick of eye, fertile in expedients, ftrong of hand, active of foot, and fearlefs in execution. His fturdy, well-built figure, ruddy complexion, and frank open countenance, as feen upon his tomb, are at once an evidence and an effect of this trait, which is further attefted by tradition and his writings. He was fond of fociety, anxious to have a ftately, well-appointed houfe and eftablifhment, a little proud of his gentle blood, and ready with the firſt joke that came uppermoſt to tickle Southampton, retaliate upon Ben Jonſon, or make John-a-Combe chuckle.

Next, he was totally free from the pedantry of an author. He looks neither mad, nor ſentimental, nor melancholy, nor inſpired. While ſmaller men are apt to magnify the value of works which have coſt them immenſe labour and effort to produce, he cared ſo little for the ſpontaneous productions of his genius that he took no care about them once they had anſwered their immediate purpoſe. The ordinary companions of his later days were the honeſt ſquires and burghers of War- wickſhire, nor do the few jokes recorded of him at all ſmell of the lamp, but rather refer to the purſuits of ordinary men. All his aims were practical. His object in life was to ſecure to himſelf an independence, and to enjoy the amuſements and the occupations to which his ſimple taſtes impelled him. For this purpoſe he was not too proud to turn his hand to any honeſt em- ployment, to hold gentlemen's horſes, act, adapt other men's works to the ſtage, write the fineſt plays that ever were conceived by mortal man, buy and ſell malt, and farm impropriate tithes.

As might have been expected from a man of this mould, he was free from the petty jealouſies of litera-

ture. The irritable race of his fellow poets ufe refpecting him fome turn of phrafe or epithet which denotes
perfonal affection, fuch as " gentle." Spenfer, Drayton,
Chettle, all have a kind word for him. And this is
the more fignificant, inafmuch that they muft have felt
that he had beaten them. The only exception to this
rule is Greene, who feems to me to have been the very
type of all that is moft bafe and degraded in literary
men. The irritable, overbearing, and impulfive Jonfon
declares that he loved him almoft to idolatry.

Behind thefe moral qualities rifes the ftupendous
edifice of his genius; but indeed they add much to its
beauty and effect. His manly, generous, unaffected,
and nature-loving mind is apparent in every ftone of
the ftructure—a proof, if any were wanting, that every
work of the artift is the product of his whole nature,
by which the height, depth, length, breadth, and
colour of his foul and fpirit are meafured and gauged.

And happy it was for England that our greateft Poet
was of this temperament. Who can fay what effect
the widely-fpread ftudy of his works may have on the
national character? His tranfcendent genius, had it
been combined with fome morbid fentimentalifm or
effeminate affectation, muft have more or lefs injured
the moral fenfe of the thoufands of his countrymen
to whom his writings are as familiar as houfehold

words. Lord Byron, with very inferior powers, was able actually to make it fashionable for a time to ape the maudlin egotism and weak misanthropy of a worn-out voluptuary. But there was no perverse quality in Shakespere's mind to throw a jaundiced tinge over his pictures of God's fair creation. He has shown that robust good sense is an element of the highest poetry, and that to be a great poet it is not necessary to be either mad or bad. Again, with respect to language, had he been a bookish man and a scholar, as scholarship was in those days, he would probably have fallen in with the affectations of Sir Philip Sydney, and written in the half French, half Latin jargon of the Euphuists, or tied himself to the tail of Terence and Seneca, like Jonson. Or, rebelling against the pseudo-classical mania, he might have affected archaisms, like Spenser. But instead of this, he wrote in the strong homely language of the English people of his own time; and his writings, combined perhaps with the English translation of the Bible, have fixed our language for ever. There is in them always a model, ready to our hand and familiar to everybody, of the very best colloquial English.

He has conferred another great boon upon English literature. He has created a school of dramatic criticism founded upon nature and the national character, and not upon arbitrary laws of precedents. Ariftotle laid down, and the dramatifts of Greece and Rome followed, certain canons called the Unities, which required that the action of a play fhould not occupy more than one day at moft; that the fcene fhould not change to any place fo diftant that the actors might not have reached it in the time occupied by the events reprefented ; and that in tragedy, none but tragic and dignified perfonages fhould be introduced. In one of his plays, " The Tempeft," Shakefpere has actually, whether intentionally or by accident, obferved the firft two of the Unities. The whole bufinefs of the play is tranfacted in *Profpero's* little ifland within the fpace of a few hours. It is impoffible to deny that the refult upon a reader's mind—at leaft upon a critical reader's mind—is a certain feeling of artiftic completenefs. But this advantage is not enough in general to compenfate for the bondage under which the poet who writes under thefe conditions labours. In none of Shakefpere's plays is the third Unity obferved. Whether the Greek mind, in which thefe rules originated, were fo fenfitive as not to admit the mixture of tragic and comic emotions, or whether the religious character of the Greek feftivals excluded it, or whatever may have been the origin of the canon, it certainly deprives the artift of one great inftrument of artiftic effect—contraft. The grave fcene in " Hamlet," the

scenes on the heath in "Lear," and at the castle-gate
in "Macbeth," would suffer considerably if any classical
enthusiast were to omit the parts of the gravedigger,
the fool, and the porter. At any rate, tragedy, comedy,
and farce, are strangely blended in real life, to which
Shakespere held the mirror, and our sluggish northern
imaginations require the stimulus of the contrast.
The builders of our cathedrals must carve a sow playing on the bagpipes, or a friar putting a goose into his
sleeve, on the moulding of a structure which awes the
lightest imagination by its solemn and mysterious
beauty. If Shakespere had been a scholar, we should
probably have known no tragedy but such as the
stilted productions of Corneille and Racine, or dramatic
criticism but such as Voltaire's.

And now one word upon the Tercentenary Festival.
As long as human nature remains what it is, the mind
will attach a certain sentimental importance to anni-
versaries and other epochs which recall the memory of
great events, of which the birth of Shakespere is most
assuredly one of the greatest. It is a principle inter-
woven in our religion, our laws, and our customs.
The desire to show respect to the memory of a great
man by erecting a monument to his honour is also a
natural feeling which we inherit from our Celtic,
Teutonic, or Scandinavian ancestors, whose cairns and

barrows fupply food for the fpeculations of our antiquarian focieties. But in all our attempts as a nation to
keep anniverfaries or erect monuments, we are fingu-
larly unhappy. We fet about fuch matters *moult
triftement*. Something of courfe will be done at the
coming Tercentenary Feftival, and the beft way not to
be difappointed is not to expect much. A ftatue or an
obelifk more or lefs will make little difference in the
beauty or uglinefs of our public places. Fortunately he
whom we delight to honour may fay, *Exegi monumen-
tum ære perennius*. His plays, unlike the victories of
warriors, are his real monument, and it feems to me
that through them we can beft evince our gratitude to
their author. To found a theatre in which the Shakefperian drama could be acted and a fchool of acting
maintained, would be a work really worthy of the
occafion. The difficulties in the way, though great,
are not infurmountable. There is the Academy of
Mufic in Paris endowed by the State; and in every
principal town in Italy, till lately, fome fuch home was
provided for the lyric drama. Why, then, fhould not
perfons co-operate to found a fchool of national dramatic poetry in this country? There can be no doubt
that a public which can be drawn together to hear
ftupid lectures and orations about things in general by
popular preachers, would flock to hear Shakefpere's

plays declaimed exactly as they were written, and that
without any of the factitious attractions of elaborate
fcenery and dreffes. People do not from choice feed
upon garbage when they can get wholefome food.
To hope that fuch an idea will be actually carried out
amidft the jarring elements of the literary and artiftic
world may perhaps be Utopian; but I cannot help
thinking that to provide for the adequate reprefentation
of Shakefpere's plays, and to enlarge the circle of thofe
who receive from them benefit and delight, would be
the moft rational and nobleft homage we could pay to
his greatnefs.

FINIS.

J. E. TAYLOR, PRINTER, 10, LITTLE QUEEN STREET.

www.ingramcontent.com/pod-product-compliance
Lightning Source LLC
Chambersburg PA
CBHW020105030726
47498CB00006B/1965